His eyebrows quirked with emotion. "I don't want to take anything from you, darlin'. In fact, I'm here to return somethin'." He presented her clowning glove.

She grumbled, snatching the glove from him. "Miss Limb to you, Wayne Dunbar." She said his name with all the malice that she could muster and crossed her arms. "Now, what do you want?"

He held out the rose again. "Ask you on a date, is all."

"I don't date." Sort of true. She hadn't dated in a long while and she was okay with that. In fact, she favored it because men were trouble and Wayne Dunbar was far more trouble than she'd ever consider taking on.

"Correction." He took a step closer to her. "You didn't date. Now you do."

She laughed. "Presumptuous fiend," she murmured, finding her shoes and forcing the smile to stay at bay. "Listen. Even if I did date, which I don't, I wouldn't date you."

"Why not?" He honestly looked offended, which made her fight an all-out laugh.

"Because I'm not sure I-I even like you." Also, sort of true. He was a devilish temptation with his sun-bleached waves tossed about on his head, scruffy facial hair and handsome grey eyes that always seemed to catch the light in a way that made her insides unsteady. He, however, was the reason why she was in the financial pickle she was in and she wasn't so easy to forget that.

ALEXANDRIA ASHCROFT

A DESERT ROGUE NOVEL
IMPOSSIBLE ROGUE

Black Quill Publishing LLC

Impossible Rogue by Alexandria Ashcroft

Published by Black Quill Publishing LLC Madison, WI USA

www.blackquillpublishingllc.com

This is a work of fiction. Names, characters, businesses, places, events, locales, and incidents are either the products of the author's imagination or used in a fictitious manner. Any resemblance to actual persons, living or dead, or actual events is purely coincidental.

Cover by Alexandria Ashcroft.

Author bio Pic by: Glimpse in Time Photography
Editing by: Black Quill Publishing LLC

Print Book ISBN: 978-1-949294-16-3

This book is dedicated to the consistent and persistent pursuit of your heart.

| 1 | Flower in a Barrel |

Wayne ducked into the barrel right when the angry bull's hooves pounded past.

Holy shit! The big beast barely missed him. Had it not been for the damn rodeo clown, he'd be digging horns out his ass.

"Wooo!" he howled. His voice vibrated off the walls of the barrel. He flexed his right hand and grimaced. He had to get back to the barn to wrap it up again. Doctor had warned him about it gettin' *ten-dans-itis* or somethin' other.

Another body joined him in the barrel right before the sound of the bull's hooves stomped past again.

He frowned as, under the smell of sweat and dirt, a floral scent wafted up to his nostrils. He brought his attention to the rodeo clown that was crammed in the barrel with him. It was hard to tell under the stark white makeup in the dark space whether he was seeing what he was smellin'. Surely no rodeo clown he'd ever met smelled like a young spring morning.

He reached out, touching the clown's chest. His gut clenched when his finger sank into soft flesh.

"What the fuck you doin', man?" The clown smacked his hand away.

He wasn't the greatest at vocal recognition, but if he wasn't mistaken—

"You're a *chick*?!"

5

She let out a long exhale before poking her head out of the barrel.

He wasn't sure why he was so excited. Maybe because it was just so unexpected. He was certain he'd never heard of, or better yet seen, a lady rodeo clown. "You are, aren't you?! What's your name, sweetheart?"

She rolled her eyes as she pushed her weight out and over the edge of the container.

"Hey, wait!" He wiggled out of the tight space, but when he poked his head up, he couldn't tell where his fragrant clown had gone.

He jogged out of the pen, removing his riding gloves, his eyes darting this way and that. He saw a cluster of clowns hanging around outside the pen.

"Wayne." It was his agent, Kyle, who distracted him from his mission to find that damn clown. The man had a worried look on his face as was per usual. "You did good in there, but Jason Brocker might beat you. You're losing grip on that hand." Kyle paused, which made Wayne look at him.

The thinkin' type, that Kyle, with his rimless glasses and straight symmetrical features. Always looked too cleaned up, if you asked Wayne.

"What?"

"Did you ever think that maybe you're, uh, getting a bit old for this? There are tons of other things you can do—"

"Stop right there. First off, I'm only thirty-seven.—"

"Way older than the other rid—"

"Second," he talked over the man. "I'm going to die in that pen. You hear me? There's nothing else besides the rodeo."

"Wayne, be reasonable—"

"Reasonin' is for you. Now, be a good boy, and find me another competition to ride in." Wayne clapped the man hard on the shoulder and took minor comfort in his grimace.

Wayne turned and made his way to the barn to get his horse ready his next competition.

Too old?

Who does the man think he's talking to? Wayne massaged his shoulder. He'd probably have to ice that.

"You're getting old."

He grumbled when he saw his sister, Joey Lou, in the barn brushing down the horse he was set to ride soon in the lasso. "Not you too."

She shrugged "If I lie to you, then who'll ever tell you the truth?"

He flopped down on a bale of hay. "You know where my wrist wrap's at?"

She nodded and strolled over to a bag hanging on the wall. "You'd leave your ass if it wasn't attached to your backside."

"'Least you can tell the difference between my ass and the front part of me that speaks." He waved her off and took the wrapping from her.

Joey Lou laughed so hard she snorted. "Pretty original, shit head. Remember, I'm gonna be in late in the mornin'."

He frowned. "Cleanin' that school again?"

She nodded. "I need the extra cash."

"Joey Lou, seriously, I've told you time again. I make more money than should be legally allowed."

"Ain't mine. It's yours. I ain't gonna live off you no matter how rich you get."

He shook his head, knowing good and well he was talking to a brick wall. Stubborn as the woman she came out of, that one there.

"Hey, Wayne."

He looked up and presented a roguish smile. "Marleen. What you doin' out of the stands, baby?"

"Oh, just checkin' on you. That was a close call, don't you think? Had me on the edge of my seat. Thought I might have to nurse you back to health."

He smirked, remembering the time she'd come over in her nurse uniform to tend to his needs. "Oh, Marleen, Marleen. Whatever am I gonna do with you?"

The woman sauntered into the barn, biting on her bottom lip. "I've got a couple ideas."

7

"Disgusting," Joey Lou murmured, slipping out of the barn.

Marleen linked her arms over his shoulders and took a stance between his legs. He ran his hands up her thighs and cupped her ass through her jeans.

"Reckon I got a few ideas myself."

"Mr. Dunbar?"

Wayne looked past Marleen to find a young boy standing in the barn door opening. "Billy. What is it?"

"You've got someone lookin' for you." The boy laughed. "He's in the announcer's booth. Don't seem to like the heat much."

"Good boy," Wayne said, tucking the wrapping around his wrist. "I'll be there in a minute."

"Uh, Mr. Dunbar?" Billy continued, his gaze focused on the ground as he dug his boot into the dirt.

"Yeah, son?"

"My school is havin' a car wash next weekend, and it'd mean a big deal if you'd stop by."

The corner of Wayne's mouth lifted. "Sure thing there, Billy."

"Really! You will?"

Wayne laughed a little at how high the boy's voice got. "If Wayne Dunbar says so, then it is so."

"Alright!" The little boy jumped in the air and ran out of the barn, shouting after another kid, no doubt his friend.

Wayne brought his attention back to Marleen, who was gazing down at him like he was the Messiah come back to life. "You're such a good role model."

He shrugged. "I remember when I was his age."

She rubbed his shoulders. "You didn't have to do what you did. It's so sexy."

"Yeah?"

"Mhm," she cooed. "Let me show you how sexy I think it is."

His eyes closed when she rubbed down the front of his jeans and nibbled his ear.

He groaned and grabbed her hands, reluctantly stopping her. "I'm gonna have to take a rain check, sweetheart."

She pulled back with a pout.

"Apparently someone's waiting for me."

She smirked. "It's tough being the man, ain't it?"

He pushed himself to his feet and headed toward the open barn door. "Even tougher walkin' away from someone as pretty as you." She waved him off with a shy smile, emphasizing her heavily made-up face.

"After, maybe I can stop by your loft and bring by some home cookin'?" She offered.

"Can hardly say no to that." The woman'd been to the place he rented over the town bakery many times before.

He was deep in thought when the crowd's gasp made him look up. There, on the top of the pen wall, was his clown. She jumped down and did a tuck and roll maneuver on the safe side of the pen followed by cheers and hoots from the crowd. She stood, a satisfied smile on her face, and dusted off her outfit before looking up. The smile on her painted face fell into a scowl when she met his eyes.

"Hey!" he called after her, but she made a sharp U-turn in the opposite direction. "Would you stop runnin'! Hey—" If she thought she was going to outrun him, she was mistaken. His favorite pastime, second only to riding, was chasing. He'd never chased a clown before, but there was a first time for everything.

"Wayne Dunbar." A tall, heavy set man with a southern accent blocked his path. Wayne came to a sudden halt so as not to run into the man, which Wayne figured might be much like hitting a brick wall. The man patted the beads of sweat on his forehead with a soaked handkerchief. "It's nice to meet you." He shook Wayne's hand, forcing their eyes to meet.

"I thought you were waiting in the announcer's booth." He tried to look past the man to see if his clown was still in eyesight, but the man was just too big an obstacle.

"I'm pressed for time. Let me be brief. I'm Clive Nore with Berkanville Marketing. We handle commercial campaigns for big name brands, and we have a couple brands looking at you."

Wayne frowned, finally bringing his full attention to the man. "Me?"

"You shouldn't be surprised. You've won several gold medals, always making headlines with your near stints with death. Oh, and probably the most important one is that everyone is in love with your tense relationship with Rage, the bull. I'm sure you don't need me to say you're most popular with the ladies as well." He patted his forehead again. "I'd prefer to talk in more acclimate environmental conditions. I'll be in touch through your agent with details, but I did want to meet you face to face."

"Yeah, sounds good. Kyle handles all that type of stuff. Thanks for coming out." Wayne looked past the man, but to no surprise, his clown wasn't anywhere to be found.

It didn't make no never mind. He'd find her. How many female rodeo clowns could there be?

| 2 | A Flower's Thorns |

"None."

Wayne frowned, massaging his wrist. "You sure?" He winced.

"Ain't no lady clowns. I know. I hire all of 'em."

Wayne rubbed his wrist. He needed to re-wrap it. That had been his first thought after he dominated in first place, as usual. His dismount was a bit off, caught his wrist up. As if it didn't already have problems. He brought his attention back to the greasy-haired man in front of him. "I'm sure you have a grueling vetting process."

"Oh, yeah, we clowns have a 401k, insurance and profit sharin'. You know, every fuckin' thing."

Wayne pursed his lips at the man's sarcasm. "Think real careful."

The man tossed the cigarette butt on the ground and squashed it, tapping his chin. "Naw. Don't know no lady clowns. 'Sides, what dame would be fool enough to take on a 2,400-pound beast, anyhow?"

Wayne was wondering the same thing. He presented a tight-lipped smile, understanding that he was going nowhere with the man. He turned on his heels and headed towards his truck.

He adjusted the wrap on his wrist to scratch the irritated skin under it. He was pissed to no end that he had to wear the damn thing anyway. Now it had to itch on top of it all?

He slammed the door once inside and unraveled the cloth wrapped around his wrist then proceeded to re-wrap it.

He'd been after an answer about his fragrant clown for over a week. It was proving to be more challenging than he had expected, and he wasn't really sure why he was still pursuing her. He started up the truck and pulled out of the parking lot.

Until that moment, it hadn't dawned on him that she might be trying to avoid him. He could tell his attention was not welcome, and that, for some reason, made him want to track her down even more. It went against his cowboy persona, which he was proud to live up to on a day-to-day basis. He was the one who was evasive, difficult and mysterious, not the other way around. Perhaps the switch of roles is what bothered him most. There was something refreshing about it all.

As he turned onto the street the elementary school was on, he saw a few cars being washed, one that was pulling off and a bunch of children having a good time while doing little to no work.

It dawned on him that he had promised little Billy he'd stop by the car wash. He pulled into the parking lot and upon climbing out of his truck, he immediately got the outpouring of love that he was growing accustomed to. He rarely thought of himself as a celebrity, but any sort of any kind of stardom, if you'd call it that, made everyone want to know you in his small Texas town.

Someone behind him cleared her throat, eliciting groans from the children that surrounded him asking him questions. The reluctantly returned to their tasks. He turned around and paused, taking in the beautiful brown woman's fetching features. She had big, dark, brown eyes, long curled lashes and full lips. Her tight curls were pulled back with a handkerchief. She shoved a soapy sponge into his chest.

"Gear up, Dunbar."

He laughed, more at her scowl than at what she said. "Paying and washing? What the hell am I paying for?"

"The experience," she answered blandly. "Hell you doin' with this truck anyway? You think you could have gotten any more mud on it? Hey Jen!" The woman cupped her free hand and yelled.

Another woman popped up from a crouched position on the other side of a soapy sedan. When she met Wayne's eyes, her face lit up.

Shit. He thought.

Jennifer Tauge. She'd been trying to get rid of her last name since high school, when everyone called her Tug Boat Jen. She'd lost a lot of weight since then, thanks to yold-ga, or somethin' 'nother.

"Wayne." She flounced over. "I didn't know you were stopping over. Here, let me take that sponge. You're a paying customer. You shouldn't be working." She leaned into him. "At least not working on this car anyway."

Subtle, he thought.

"Not why I called you over here."

He glanced over at the car-cleaning dictator, who looked particularly annoyed.

Jen brought her attention to the pretty brown-skinned woman next to him. "Call the fire department, 'cause I don't know how we're going to get this one clean."

The other woman waved her off. "Oh, it's nothing, Dellie!" Jen squealed. "We've got hoses and big strong men here. It's no big deal."

"Oh my God. Did you really just say big strong men? Give me that." The brown-skinned woman snatched the sponge. "And don't call me Dellie." She whistled and a bunch of little children came running over to her like she was the pied piper. "Listen up, soldiers!" she shouted.

"Ma'am, yes, ma'am," they responded in unison.

She continued. "We've got a messy situation that needs our utmost attention." A couple of girls giggled and pointed at him, whispering to each other.

Wayne smiled, crossed his arms and watched the stern woman walk the line of young people with her arms held behind her back. "Do you see this?" She pointed to his truck, which from his new vantage point indeed looked like a wretch. He'd make him clean it too, if he were her.

The children agreed, loudly.

"This is a big, huge, gigantic problem, but we don't run from problems now, do we?"

"No, ma'am, no!" the little people shouted, barely able to maintain their struggling formation as they filled with excitement.

"No, we don't. We face our problems with—"

13

"Discipline, determination and decisive action," they responded again in unison.

Amusement found him as he sat back and enjoyed the pep talk.

"That's right." She stopped pacing and faced them, her stance wide and secure. He ventured to guess she had spent some time serving in the military. He wondered which division. Army, if he had to guess. He had more admiration for the woman with that discovery.

Wayne looked around and saw near everyone was looking at the woman pump up her little army. He scratched his facial hair, content with watching the beautiful woman work her magic.

"Our plan, once executed, will yield us a hefty tip." She glanced back at him with an accusatory, raised eyebrow. "That plan is—" She held out the word. "Clean, clean, clean, clean!!!" The young people took off, grabbing buckets, and water, hoses, and sponges. Fully armed, they all attacked the truck.

His gaze fell on the woman, who had a slight smile on her face as she labored on the taller parts of the car that the children couldn't reach.

Goddamn, he thought. *If my heart didn't already belong to that mysterious clown, I would be all over this woman*.

He strolled up to her and grabbed the sponge, as she was struggling to reach the very top of the truck. She took a few steps back, looking mildly offended. "It's okay, Mr. Dunbar. Would hate for you to mess up your manicure. Sit back and see what your money gets ya. We don't need your help."

"Doesn't mean I won't give it." He looked down into her deep brown eyes and his insides stirred.

Fucking gorgeous.

A waft of familiar flowers slid up his nostrils and he turned and looked behind him. He regretted it when Jen strolled up to him.

"Wayne, you really have to come to the red carpet event the children are throwing in a couple weeks. It would mean so much to them."

Wayne rubbed the back of his neck. He liked kids enough, but he didn't like to be the object of everyone's attention unless he was on a bull.

"Well, I don't know."

Jen pouted. "With a headliner like you, we could raise so much money for the children to go on field trips. So many of them, 'specially the young boys, look up to you."

He let out an uncomfortable laugh. "They really shouldn't."

"We know that." He looked over his shoulder to find the pretty military woman cleaning the top of the car with a ladder as she talked. "Doesn't stop 'em though. Wouldn't it be somethin'," she continued leaning over to get the middle of the top of the truck. "Them finding out you're just as disappointing as any other man with so much power."

He frowned and faced her, crossing his arms over his chest. She was fuckin' with his character now and that for some reason was irritating beyond ignoring. That, or maybe because he wanted her to have a different opinion of him.

He frowned because he'd never cared before.

"Dellie, agitating the man isn't going to help convince him," Jen said out of the side of her mouth, leaning toward the other woman.

Dellie, so she was called, rolled her eyes. "Don't need no convincing. Can't you see, he already made up his mind?"

He shook his head, irritated that the woman thought she knew what he was thinkin'. He didn't care that she was right. "I'll have you know, I have made up my mind. I'd love to support the kids. I'm just sorry I didn't know about it previous years." He turned his attention to Jen. "I'll be giving a hefty donation and a generous tip, because that's the kind of guy I am."

Jen squealed, jumping up and down and clapping her hands. "This is great news! Tom, Margerie, come over here. You've got to hear this!" She ventured off to share the good news with others.

The corner of his mouth lifted, feeling like he had somehow won some sparring matching with the woman Jen called Dellie. "Shows how well you know—" he broke off when he looked back toward his truck and the woman was nowhere to be found.

He frowned. *Where had she gone that fast?* He noticed the sponge, however, was still on top of the car.

"Hey Dunbar."

He turned in the direction of the pretty woman's voice and found her holding a water hose with a sinister smirk on her face.

Shit! he thought, but it was too late. She'd already blasted him with the hose.

He slipped in a puddle and found himself looking up at the blue sky. For some odd reason a laugh erupted from his middle. He squinted as the woman stood over him, blocking the sun. "Sometimes you should just leave well enough alone." She offered her hand to him, and he took it, surprised at how helpful she was at actually pulling him to stand.

"Well, aren't you a piece of work?"

She smirked and shrugged. "Piece of God's work, you better believe it."

He laughed from deep within his gut. "Mhm. My Granma'am always said the Lord had a sense of humor." He turned to his car and kept wiping it down enjoying watching the woman struggle not to smile like he could tell she wanted to. "Sometimes, pretty Miss Lady," he continued after a while. "You think you know someone and you don't."

She grunted grabbing his attention. "And sometimes," she said getting the windows with cleaner and wipin' them down. "You're right on target."

| 3 | Whisky Women & Watches |

It was an awful long ride to Dallas. Wayne felt out of place the moment the tall buildings came into view. That was, until he saw the pretty brunette behind the reception counter in the oversized entrance to the tall glass-windowed building. Kyle was talking to her, but she kept making eyes at Wayne. She presented a shy smile and he bit his lower lip. He'd have her bent over that desk before the blush left her cheeks if he had it his way.

If he really had things his way, it wouldn't have been another week with no luck finding his fragrant clown. So there he was on to the next thing.

"Thank you, Mr. Dunbar, for agreeing to come meet with us," the large man said, coming from the elevator bay, dabbing his head with a handkerchief. He interrupted Wayne's thoughts, forcing him to frown. Even in the air-conditioned building the man was sweating like a hog on a hot summer day.

The man led them to an elevator that took them up to a sleek modern conference room. The further Wayne got from the ground, the more anxious he became. People weren't meant to live in the sky. If they were, they'd have wings. That's what his mama always said when she found him on the roof. He was starting to see why she was right.

He flopped down in a leather chair facing a large ribbon of windows that filled the space with natural daylight. The dark wood table was nice, but the chrome finishes were a little too cold for his liking. He was an outdoorsy kind of guy so the air conditioning made him shiver.

The heavy man took a seat in a chair that creaked under his weight. He took two big breaths before speaking. "Liz will be in shortly. She's running a little behind from another meeting. I think you're going to be thrilled with the—"

A woman swanned into the room and interrupted him with her presence, and a phone pressed to her ear. Her platinum blonde hair was cut so she almost looked like a boy, but her body told him she was pure woman. Toned legs terminated in tall shiny black heels with deep red bottoms for soles.

"I expect an update as soon as you hear." She hung up the phone and presented a forced smile. "Mr. Dunbar." She shook his hand, then Kyle's, her grip almost as strong as his own. "A pleasure meeting you. We're all busy, so I'm going to get right to the point. We want you. More specifically, our clients want you. Enough that we'd like to sign a multi-product promotion package with you. Is that something that interests you?"

"As I explained in previous correspondences with Mr. Nore, Wayne already has lucrative endorsement campaigns with Leviticus Jeans, Salazar Salsa, and Forge's pick-up truck line, with others in the works," Kyle said, pushing his glasses on his face. The woman, however, held Wayne's gaze.

"I already spoke with those companies, and they are interested in my idea either as partners, or as buy outs. But let's keep it honest. What they're talking about is child's play compared to what I'm handing to you on a silver platter." She set back in the chair and crossed her legs. Twinkling in the depths of her deep blue eyes, he saw intelligence and intrigue. She had his attention and she knew it. The corner of his mouth pulled up. She'd only be foolin' herself if she thought he'd agree to something without having everything laid out first. Kyle had made sure to have their lawyer present as well.

The man annoyed him sometimes, but he had a good head on his shoulders.

"Well," Kyle continued. "We're here to hear you out." Wayne could hear the irritation in the man's voice. The woman didn't seem to care. She just stared at Wayne, slowly tapping her long slender forefingers against each other.

She nodded toward Mr. Nore but didn't let Wayne's eyes go. The man placed a shiny black envelope on the table and pushed it toward Kyle. Kyle opened it and reviewed its contents while the silent room seemed to close in on them.

"I-I don't understand," he said after a moment. "These are luxury brands. Not typical for a bull rider. I was thinking cigarette companies or something, but luxury watches?"

"Wayne doesn't smoke," she said blandly. "Besides, after losing my father to 'em I wouldn't represent those companies anyway." She broke eye contact for the first time and brought her attention to Kyle. "Did you get to the last page?"

Kyle frowned and kept paging through the document. His mouth fell open and he removed his glasses before meeting Wayne's eyes. Without a word he slid the folder toward Wayne.

Wayne gazed down, and it took everything in him to keep his wits about him. He was certain he'd never seen that many zeros in his life. With measured calm he paged through the folder, closed it and slid it toward the woman. "That ain't Wayne Dunbar. I'm a bull rider, not some tie-wearin' office executive."

The woman let out a forced laugh that didn't reach her eyes. "With that kind of money—"

"Ain't about the money."

"You do realize you're not going to be here for long, right?" She leaned forward, near showin' him her talons. He loved a strong woman, he did, and this one was vicious. Like a dog with a bone, and he was the bone.

"You ain't changin' me. No matter the amount of zeros. I know who I am. I know what my fans like."

"That's the point, Mr. Dunbar. You haven't even started to know who your fans are. When was the last time you were on social media?"

He frowned. "Social what?"

"Exactly." She leaned back in her chair. "Don't think of it as changing who you are, but a promotion. You've settled in your fame long enough to taste some of the finer things. Still that rough rogue who everyone loves, but with a knack for fine whisky and expensive watches."

His frown deepened. "Spinnin' a lie still makes it a lie."

"You don't have to agree with all the contracts. How about we send you home with one of the watches, a tie collection, and the leather boots. You wear them and see if you like them, and then we'll talk."

"Gonna send me home with the whisky too?"

The woman smiled. "Sure. Though it sounds like you're already on board with that one."

He shrugged, holding on tight to his nonchalance. His mama had said a lot of things when it came to negotiation, and keeping your cool was a huge one. He didn't want this woman to be able to read him. That kept her vigilant. Didn't want her to think he was on board, not quite yet. But he didn't want her to think he wasn't either. "Makes sense to me. Fits the whole cowboy theme, don't you think?"

The woman's eyes lit up and the corner of her thin, pink-painted lips lifted. "That's perfect. Mr. Nore, write that down. 'Makes sense to me.' It's simple. It's Wayne. I like it. We're building the campaign off that."

Wayne slid the black folder toward Kyle. "We'll chew on it, get back to you."

They all stood. "I'd like you to keep in mind that we'd run everything by you before making any big decisions." She shook his hand, but it was softer than the first time. "Think of it more like a partnership." He looked at the woman with a raised eyebrow, noticing how close she was and how low her voice was.

"I'll keep that in mind."

It seemed like an eternity passed before they were finally on solid ground. Wayne desperately wanted to fall to the ground and kiss it, but Kyle's solid hand on his shoulder interrupted Wayne's thoughts.

"Wayne, are you crazy? You're never gonna get a deal like that again. That kind of money would set you and your children's children up for a lifetime."

"Kyle."

"When has a country, small-town hick like you ever seen that kind of money?"

"Kyle."

The man stopped pacing and faced Wayne. "It ain't about the money, okay? It ain't. The lady was right. You're not gonna be on bulls forever. Fact is, not too much longer. If you're smart—"

"Kyle!"

"What?"

"I didn't say no, did I?"

The man exhaled but held Wayne's eyes.

"Ain't it called negotiations? If we just accept their first offer, it defeats the whole purpose of the dance."

Kyle rolled his eyes, but looked relieved. Wayne clapped him on the back. "You worry too much."

"You risk too much."

"No risk, no reward." They started walking. "My Ma always said to me: 'If'n they start with silver, and you hold, they'll surely end up givin' you gold.'" He slapped the man on the chest. "Now, let's see how these city boys do a steak."

| 4 | Flowers & Favors |

Wayne flexed his hand a few times before wrapping the rope, secured underneath the big beast, around his hand. He felt the powerful animal's body take in a breath and heard it puff through its nose.

You gotta be crazy to do what I do. He smiled inside and out, then rolled his neck. He wondered if his pretty clown would be out there.

He only assumed she was pretty, of course. Someone who smelled so good had to be, right? What about the clown make-up though, this line of work?

He shrugged. Quick cash, probably. Not a bad gig as far as pay went.

Speaking of gigs. His mind quickly wandered to the meeting in Dallas over a week ago.

The pen opened and he arched his back into the bull's bucks. He held on, feeling the adrenaline fuel him. He was the last contender. He loved that position. All he had to do was hold on a moment longer than the other guys. It was all him then. Him and the clock. He adjusted his weight as the mighty animal changed his pattern.

His insides lit up when he heard the crowd counting along with the voice in his head. He hopped off the bull once the crowd erupted in cheers and jumped over the gate to safety.

He flexed his hand and laughed. It never got old. Never failed to make him feel—

He brought his attention to the present, hearing taunting voices.

"What's the problem? It's just a cock check. Balls ain't big enough to pass?"

"Bigger than yours, I'm sure."

The taunting voices chuckled a little, but their humor wasn't sincere.

Wayne's ears perked up when he heard the forced low voice from his evasive clown.

"Ain't nowhere to go. Now spread 'em—"

"Seem to be some kind of problem here?" Wayne walked in the clearing right behind the risers. Five clowns had one surrounded. It was impossible to tell if the lone clown was his because said clown was in a different costume than he'd seen previously. But he had a hunch; like before, the costume was big and baggy on her petite body.

"Naw, Wayne, ain't no problem," one of them stammered, scratching his greasy hair.

"Go on then. Go 'n' do your job." The five rogue clowns scurried off, leaving one. When the others were out of earshot, Wayne spoke. "Can't seem to stay out of trouble, huh?" He crossed his arms over his chest and leaned casually on a metal post holding up the bleachers.

"Wouldn't be no trouble if you'd have minded your business. Now you've got these dumbasses looking for a woman rodeo clown." She cleared her throat, strained from trying to make it sound lower.

"You should have just told me your name."

"Fuck off, Wayne Dunbar." She said it with such malice he had no choice but to laugh.

"You know me?"

She scoffed. "Be a fool not to. Just leave me alone, okay?"

"What if I don't want to?" He wasn't sure why he wanted to know so bad. He was causing her issue, he saw that. That hadn't been his intention, but he also just had to find out who she was. Perhaps then he could let her go.

She squared her shoulders and held his gaze with a piercing one of her own. "I'm not your type."

"Oh, yeah? And what type is that?"

"Blonde, tanned, easy."

He frowned. *Had she seen Marleen?*

"I'm more of a deathly white," she continued, pointing to her painted face. He smiled. "Don't mind the colored hair. I just can't seem to make up my mind."

He laughed out loud. She might have been trying to shoo him away, but he was the persistent type and she had humor. He liked a woman who could make him laugh. "There's a distinct difference between a lay and a date."

She crossed her arms over her chest, pressing her clown suit to her shape enough for him to see the shadow of her breasts. "Date?" She rolled her dark eyes and wrinkled her nose behind the clown paint. "Dates don't end in the backseat of a pickup truck."

"Don't believe everything you read in the gossip column, sweetheart." He was certain he'd never met a woman quite so difficult or quite so intriguing.

Her clown smile pulled up. "Funny thing is, you really think you're different than them. What?" She adjusted her stance. "You 'save' me and you're some white knight? You're a bully all the same."

"I think you're just convinced about me already, little lady. I don't see how I'm a villain after gettin' those boys gone like I did."

"If you'd have left me alone to begin with, there would be no need for savin'.'"

"What can I say? You set up an interesting mystery."

She strolled up to him and poked him in the chest. He got a whiff of her floral scent and his heartbeat picked up. "You're fucking with my money, Wayne. I don't like that."

He grabbed her white, gloved hand. When she tried to pull away, he pressed her to him by the small of her back.

She gasped and splayed her free hand on his chest.

She glared up at him.

"Most women think I'm charming." The corner of his mouth pulled up in a roguish smile. A smile that women always complimented him on. A smile they all swooned over.

She presented a painful smile back up at him, her dark eyes boring into his soul. As close as they were, he could see a hint of her eyebrows behind the clown makeup. They were pulled together.

He chuckled. *She's mad as a bull with a rope tied 'round it's balls.* Her chest pressed against him as she dragged in a sturdy breath.

"If you're looking for most women, you have the wrong clown." She stomped his foot, shoved him hard, and turned to run. He gripped her hand, but only pulled off her glove. He frowned when she pulled away a brown-skinned appendage and spirited off toward the pen.

He raised an eyebrow with the feeling of triumph filling his chest. Shouldn't be hard to find a pretty brown woman in a small town like his. 'Sides, the Sheriff owed him a favor anyway.

| 5 | Curious Minds |

"Very good, Lucy. Roy, you're up next. Please share your essay on someone you admire."

The little boy stood with a smirk. Desiree already knew he was about to say something ignorant. He was lucky he was only in fourth grade. He held the paper up to his face.

"The person I admire the most is Wayne Dunbar." Some of the other boys traded sly smiles and comments of agreement. Desi crossed her arms and rolled her eyes. *Can I not get rid of this pest?*

"Please, share why Mr. Dunbar is so admirable," she said blandly. He was haunting her without even being there. How was that possible?

"You mean, besides him being rich, and having all the chicks?"

Laughter broke out around the room.

"Yes, besides that." She adjusted her arms and perched on the edge of her desk. Beyond his persistence, she was mad that his attention had suspended her clowning job. That was the only thing she had to help her mom. The medical bills weren't going to pay themselves, and her brother was already paying over half.

The little boy's face scrunched up in thought. "Well, he's fearless."

She raised an eyebrow. "Sometimes a healthy dose of fear is a good thing."

The little hellion smirked. "Not when you're riding a bull it ain't." Roy turned toward the class with a dramatic sway of his slender arms. He crouched over and leaned toward his classmates. As much as she didn't like the lessons about equality and racial diversity the boy learned at home, she had to admit he had an enduring quality to him. "You've got to stare 'em in the eyes and dare 'em to come at you."

"A smart rider would run to safety and let the rodeo clowns take on the beast."

The boy waved her off as if she knew nothing of the topic. "Only a coward would do that. 'Sides, clowns ain't good for nothin' no way. But they do look a hoot when the bull catches up." He made bull horns with his pointer and pinky finger, pressed them to his forehead and ran down the row of desks. The class erupted in loud chatter and some laughs at Roy's antics. He high-fived one of the other boys.

"Alright, alright, settle down." She calmed the room. "What else?"

The boy strolled back up to the front of the classroom and faced his peers. "He's daring and—" He frowned when his classmates fell silent. Their mouths fell open, many of them not blinking. They stared at the front of the room in awe.

Desi frowned herself and hesitantly started turning to see what they were looking at.

"I don't know." The man's heavy voice stopped her movement. "Those pesky rodeo clowns are pretty daring too."

She froze in place and dared not to turn and look.

"I don't believe it," Roy murmured. "Holy cows callin' home for supper. *The* Wayne Dunbar." The little boy's blue eyes sparkled as he stared at his idol.

She finally looked toward the door and saw the impossibly handsome rogue leaning on the door frame. His gaze was focused on her.

One of the girls in the front gasped. "Is the rose for Miss Limb? Aww," she cooed, joined by a couple of other girls.

"Impossible," Roy retorted, crossing his arms over his slender chest. "Wayne Dunbar's not the romantic type."

"Dear boy, there's more to a man than the rodeo," he said, his stare still focused on her.

She pushed off the desk and made her way to Wayne, ignoring the heat his deep voice made course through her blood. "I have to agree with Roy on this one. That rose is not for me. Mr. Dunbar, outside please. Class, you can study for your spelling quiz." She shoved him out the door and closed it behind her.

"What the hell are you doing here?"

He held out the rose. "This is for you."

"No, it's not!" she whispered, loudly. "Answer me."

"Why are you whisperin'?" His cool, casual southern lilt made her want to kiss the smirk off his face and slap him at the same time.

"This is my place of work," she sniped, crossing her arms. "Unless you want to take this source of income too."

His eyebrows quirked with emotion. "I don't want to take anything from you, darlin'. In fact, I'm here to return somethin'." He presented her clowning glove.

She grumbled, snatching the item from him. "Miss Limb to you, *Wayne Dunbar*." She said his name with all the malice that she could muster and crossed her arms. "Now, what do you want?"

He held out the rose again. "Ask you on a date, is all."

"I don't date." *Sort of true.* She hadn't dated in a long while and she was okay with that. In fact, she favored it because men were trouble and Wayne Dunbar was far more trouble than she'd ever consider taking on.

"Correction." He took a step closer to her. "You didn't date. Now you do."

She laughed. "Presumptuous fiend," she murmured, finding her shoes and forcing the smile to stay at bay. "Listen. Even if I did date, which I don't, I wouldn't date you."

"Why not?" He honestly looked offended, which made her fight an all-out laugh.

"Because I'm not sure I-I even like you." *Also, sort of true.* He was a devilish temptation with his sun-bleached waves tossed about on his head, scruffy facial hair and handsome grey eyes that always seemed to catch the light in a way that made her insides unsteady. He, however, was the reason why she was in the financial pickle she was in and she wasn't so easy to forget that.

He frowned. "What's not to like?"

"Haha … where to start?" She tapped her chin. "You temporarily suspended a very lucrative side hustle for me. As you can imagine, teaching isn't all that profitable and I have bills to pay. We can add stalking me at my job, and unsolicited touches for feelin' me up in that barrel."

He laughed, a sound she didn't want to enjoy. "You'll get your side job back. Those boneheads will forget all about it soon as they forgot their wit right out the womb."

She failed at not smiling at that. "That's the only thing that's keeping you in one piece right now. I can't wait for those dim wits to get out of my way, so I've had to make other arrangements." She had picked up tutoring nights and weekends, but she didn't tell him that.

Her eyes darted down the hall to some people heading their way. "You should go."

"I can't do that. I'm truly sorry to hear about your struggles, but I can't leave without gettin' what I came for."

She didn't need to ask him what he came for. She already knew. Unfortunately, she wasn't so willing to give him that which he thought he could have in the first place. She frowned and squared her shoulders, taking a step toward him. He looked down to meet her

28

glaring eyes. "You're used to dealing with bulls, Mr. Dunbar. I'm far worse."

"That so?" She heard the amusement in the man's heavy voice. "Why would you venture to say that?"

"The worst they can do to you is put some horns in your ass." She glared for emphasis. "I'm not interested in dating you. Please, leave."

The corner of his mouth lifted. "Guess I'll see you at the fundraiser tomorrow night, then. Save me a dance."

"Don't hold your breath," she said as she slipped back into her classroom.

| 6 | To Save a Rogue a Dance |

Wayne cut the engine.

He had seen pretty Miss Limb walk into the elementary school's gym when he pulled into the parking lot. It didn't much matter to him that as soon as she saw him, she looked forward and started walking fast as if he'd come to snatch her purse or somethin'.

Truth was, he had been regretting the entire thing until the moment he saw her. Kyle had said it'd be a good thing showin' up and raisin' money for the kids. He liked kids well enough, but he didn't like being the star of the show unless he was on a buckin' bull. The only reason he had really agreed was because the little firecracker Miss Limb had put him in a pickle at the car wash. The woman had a way about her, she did, and he liked it.

It had hurt his ego a little bit when she flat out turned him down the day before, but looking back, maybe he hadn't handled things the best. He should have bought her an entire bouquet of flowers. *Did she like roses? Maybe something a little more robust next time?*

He made his way inside and was shocked when he was confronted with flashing lights and a red carpet made out of a collage of red colored pieces of paper. It had obviously been crafted by the children. He was bombarded with a microphone, hands and arms around his shoulders, a slender bony hand sliding into his and leading him further inside. He looked down and found Jen's bright, clear blue eyes.

"Welcome to the Clispin Elementary Grand Gala." He looked around to see the decorations had also all been handmade by the children. Many adults mingled around with cups of punch, chatting in pockets around the gym. He brought his attention back to Jen as she started talking to the local news guy. "All the proceeds will go to the children's various trips throughout the year. It gives them an opportunity to leave the classroom and explore. And our biggest contributor is Mr. Wayne Dunbar!"

Wayne nodded at the man.

"What made you decide to contribute so generously?"

A woman that goes by pretty Miss Limb. He cleared his throat. "Young people shouldn't be trapped in classrooms. There's a world out there for 'em and if a few dollars will help them get out there, then I did my job."

"Hardly just a few dollars..." Jen continued on, swelling up his contribution better than he could on his best day. It was fine by him anyway, because then his attention could be pulled across the room to a small cluster of people near the punch. Miss Limb was talking casually before her eyes caught his. She looked away and crossed her arms before pulling some loose curls behind her ear.

He smirked.

She looked irritated to see him. Irritation meant she was trying not to feel what she was really feeling for him and he knew she felt something. His instincts were rarely wrong. That's why he was a great bull rider.

Before he could settle on Miss Limb's subtle beauty, Jen pulled him along, introducing him to people whose names and faces he wouldn't ever remember because his attention was elsewhere.

His beautiful desert flower kept moving throughout the evening, seeming to always be on the opposite side of the room. When Jen was finally pulled away for somethin' or another, he shook out his wrinkled shirt sleeve and made a beeline to his evasive target. Her back was to him, which was perfect. Meant she couldn't slip away.

"Excuse me." His fingers tingled as they grazed over her silky, soft skin. Goosebumps rose on the flawless surface following his touch. It did somethin' to him, knowin' he had an effect on her even if she wouldn't admit it. "May I steal her away for a dance?" He hadn't actually noticed the music before as he'd tuned out all sound in order to free his mind from Jen's high-pitched voice that seemed to reach octaves he didn't even know were possible.

The other two people with her nodded and slipped away, leaving her with a look of betrayal on her face. He placed a hand on her back and led them to the dance floor with a number of others who had grabbed a partner and were swaying to a slow country song.

He let his fingers rest on her lower back while he made his way to face her. She put one hand on his shoulder and let him take her other hand in his. She kept her eyes averted while he pulled her closer and started swaying. He made damn sure to keep his sweatin' palms up high. He didn't want to piss the evasive woman off. Not just yet, anyway.

She looked so pretty. Being close to her, he could smell her soft floral scent. His mouth started to water as his mind wandered, curious if she tasted like flowers too.

He cleared his throat and his mind. The worst thing to happen right now would be for him to get a hard-on while dancing with her. That'd be sure to scare her off or worse. He examined her face. Even in the dim lighting her skin looked flawless. He wondered if she was wearing make-up or if she just always looked that way.

She glanced up at him for a moment and he saw her dark brown eyes, framed by thick black lashes. Her full lips relaxed a little bit, making his eyes fall to her mouth. He just wanted to kiss her right then and there.

He looked away for a moment. When he found her face again, her gaze was averted again.

"I almost expected you not to come."

He frowned down at her. "I might be a lot of things pretty Miss Limb deems distasteful, but one thing I am not is a flake. I said I'd be here; so, here I am."

She adjusted her hand on his shoulder, bringing it closer to his neck. He found her warm gaze again. "Good to know there's at least one redeeming quality about you."

The corner of his mouth pulled up at her jab. "To what end?"

She frowned up at him. "Excuse me?"

He smiled, joy filling him just from being in her presence. "What's the point of something good if it doesn't yield you your reward?"

She looked away from him and exhaled. "Looks like I spoke too soon."

"What? I can't have many reasons why I do something?"

"To answer your question, the point of doing something good is just to do something good. Not to do something for a reward, but because you believe in it."

Such passion. He wondered if she was so fiery in bed. "Oh darlin', I don't do nothin' I don't believe in. I meant what I said about the kids gettin' out. I hated learnin' from books myself."

She let silence settle between them again. It killed him not knowin' what she was thinking. She looked up at him, her eyes searching his face. A slight smile pulling up the corner of her full lips.

Damn, she's an angel.

"There just might be hope for you yet, Wayne Dunbar."

His chest filled with warmth at hearing those words from her. He hadn't realized he was looking for her approval until that moment.

He put her hand around his waist, pulling her closer and cupping her cheek.

"W-wayne." Her voice was breathy and low enough to stir his solemn innards. Her startled brown eyes met his.

"You look beautiful." He stroked her cheek with his thumb. "Fancy dresses seem to suit you."

"Thank you," she said plainly, pulling away from him.

"I've got a fancy to do comin' up—"

"Wayne, oh God. Sorry to...uh... interrupt," Jen whispered loudly, poking her head into his view. "I need to steal Wayne a moment. You don't mind, do you, Desi?" The woman didn't wait for Miss Limb to respond. Instead, she just hooked her arm in the crook of his arm and guided him away. "We need to take pictures with you in front of the display with some of the kids."

"Can't we after this song?" He noticed the coolness of his flower's absence and he stopped walking capturing Jen's attention.

"Ooooh, I'm afraid it can't wait. Todd is leaving soon to prepare for his segment tonight. It'll only take a minute."

"Fine," he grumbled. "Just give me—" He frowned when he looked to his side to find his thorny flower had, yet again, slipped from his grasp. He looked around, but the woman was nowhere to be seen.

His frown deepened. *She's good. Damn good.* He'd give her that, but he was better.

| 7 | Gettin' Him Gone |

"Hey Limb!"

Desi was startled out of her thoughts as she came out of the bathroom. The kids were probably already back from recess. "Aubrey. Hey. What's up?"

"Remember at the gala you mentioned the Monster Truck show coming to town?"

Desi nodded with a smile. "Oh yeah! Love those things."

Aubrey giggled. "So do I. We should go."

"Yeah, that'd be great. Hey, text me the info. My hooligans just came in from recess."

"Oh, yeah better get back to 'em for they put glue in your chair or something! I'll text you."

Desi breezed away with a smile. She was grateful for Aubrey. She had started a few years before Desi was hired. She was so down to earth and fun. It had been easy for them to find lots of things in common.

She breezed into the room and wrote two words on the board.

"Today we're going to talk about the difference between 'worst' and 'worse.'"

She turned to the class. "The definition of 'worse" is something of lower quality or a lower standard. It is a comparative adjective which is used to differentiate two things in relationship with each other. Like—"

35

"This lesson is the worse."

The class started giggling and whispering. Desi stilled her insides when she heard the man's familiar voice. It was low and gravelly and made her blood heat up. She stood straight when she saw the irritating rogue leaning against the doorframe. He casually looked at her as if he had every right to be there, again.

Arrogant man!

"Actually, no, Mr. Dunbar. That would be an example of how to use 'worst,' which is defined as 'of the lowest quality or the lowest standard.' The proper way to use 'worse' would be something like, 'your grammar is worse than your timing.'"

Some of her students giggled as more whispers started around the room.

His smirk widened and he strolled into the classroom, pointing at the vase on her desk. "I see my flower found its home."

"Indeed. Is that why you're here?"

Confusion made the man's eyebrows twist. "What you mean?"

"Have you lost your way home? Is that how you ended up here?"

The corner of his mouth pulled up further, revealing some teeth. "Nah, I'm right where I need to be."

She frowned and crossed her arms over her chest. The man had no concept of rude, disrespectful, unwelcome. He just strolled on in as if he had every right, as if he was invited, as if he owned the place. What the hell was security protocol for this type of insanity? She supposed this was the price she paid for taking a job in the middle of nowhere.

"I advise you to come up with a good reason as to why you're interrupting my class."

"Say, kids," Wayne turned toward them before perching on the edge of her desk. "Y'all wanna hear a story? It's highly educational, I promise."

To her annoyance, but not her surprise, they encouraged him. "This'll be about the 'worst' time I had ridin'. It was when I got my spur stuck in the strap. That beast was buckin' somethin' fierce tryin' to lose me. The only thing that saved me was that the spur broke. I rolled off the beast just in time, though it near stomped me right in the chest. I barely managed to get out of the way."

"Ah, you're fearless!" Roy said, enthralled by the man's story.

He pushed off the desk and made his way over to the boy. "No, son, I was very afraid, but I didn't let that stop me." He crouched down to meet the little boy's eyes. "Say, young man. Tell me, what would you say to an ornery bull with its horns pointed straight at you?"

"Nothin'." The little boy smirked. "I'd stare it right in the eyes and think, *you're mine.*"

Wayne's heavy laughter filled the room. "I like you, boy. You remind me of me."

The little boy's eyes glistened as he gazed up at his hero while the man got to his feet again. "Hey Mr. Dunbar, can you sign my boot? I wore these to my first rodeo. You won first place, smoked 'em by a long shot."

Wayne laughed and pulled something from his pocket. "I'll do you one better." He handed the boy something, and his little eyes lit up, examining it. "My lucky spur."

"The one from your story!"

Wayne nodded.

Desi cleared her throat, ignoring the warmth that filled her chest. "Back to your desk, Roy."

"But Miss Limb..."

"You'd rather do some writing over recess instead?"

The boy grumbled and headed to his desk.

"Get out your math work books."

Everyone groaned.

"The show's over. Mr. Dunbar is leaving now." She ushered Wayne to the door. "Pages 24 to 30. Work alone. I'll be back in a second."

She closed the door after them. "You would deprive these young minds of a teacher?" She crossed her arms over her chest. "That's what's going to happen if you keep showin' up unannounced."

"You're not gonna lose your job. Principal Dean and I go way back." He smirked, matching her stance.

She growled. "Your relationship with Principal Dean does not concern me. You gettin' me fired does."

"Won't take much to get me gone," he said, holding her eyes with a steady calm as if he were looking a bull in the eyes. "If you hadn't slipped out on me last night, I would have gotten the chance to ask you out like I was plannin' to."

She rolled her eyes, mostly to dispel the flapping butterfly wings in her stomach. She crossed her arms and leaned nonchalantly against the wall. "When's the damn date?"

His handsome face pulled into an obnoxious but charming smile, joy filling his eyes. "Tonight at eight. I'll pick you up."

"Can't. I'm traveling to Houston."

He frowned. "When do you get back?"

"Sunday."

She ignored the buoyant feeling in her chest when a smile broke out on his face. It made his grey eyes dance with triumph.

"Eight o'clock Sunday then. I'll pick you up."

"Seven, and I'll meet you there."

"Seven, and I'll pick you up."

She raised an eyebrow. "Seven. I'll meet you there."

He laughed. "That's not how negotiations work, honey."

"You've never negotiated with me—" She gasped when he trapped her between the classroom door and his body by putting his arms on either side of her.

"Seven and I'll pick you up," he said, his breath whispering over her lips. She smelled mint and a hint of tobacco. His eyes were holding hers. She could feel her body gravitate toward his strong, masculine energy.

"You can pick me up here," she countered, hating the airy quality of her voice. It exposed her weakness, and she didn't like that one bit. Not when it came to Wayne. She knew he was a problem and she had to get rid of him fast. The issue was, he wasn't easy to get rid of.

"What?" He frowned. "You think I'm gonna burn down your house or somethin'?"

38

She put a hand on his chest and extended her arm, pushing him away. She needed the space. "I don't want some stalking stranger knowing where I live." She turned and put her hand on the door handle. "Don't be late." She walked back into her classroom, trying to gain her cool back, trying to slow her breathing and steady her shaking hands.

She looked up as she entered, noticing the space was too quiet. She frowned and closed the door behind her, looking at her class.

"What's going on?"

Snickers started breaking out in the room.

It was Stacey Evans who spoke up. "He's so handsome and he obviously likes you."

"Wayne Dunbar don't need to be traipsin' after some schoolteacher." She startled when Roy's voice came from behind her. She glared at him and crossed her arms watching him stroll back to his desk. "He can have any girl he wants."

"Well, perhaps if you tell him, he'll listen," she grumbled under her breath.

"Shut up Roy!" Stacy interjected. "'Sides, shouldn't it mean more that he can have any girl, and he wants Miss Limb?" Stacey cooed, trading dreamy-eyed smirks with a couple of girls around her.

The boy flopped in his seat and exhaled. "I'm sorry to be the one to break it to you, Miss Limb, but I'd hate for my favorite teacher to get her heart broken."

Favorite teacher? I wasn't expecting that. Desi shook her head at the boy and raised an eyebrow. "Since you've so much wisdom to in part on us today, why don't you do the first math problem on the board?"

The boy whined.

"Ah, ah, ah, I don't want to hear it. Kevin, you're next. Come on, take the marker and start working through the problem."

Anything to change the subject. Wasn't it bad enough that she had to face the miscreants every day in class? With the town being so small, she was certain everyone would know before school let out about her plans with Wayne sunday. Rumors would start to fly, she just knew it.

As much as she wanted to slap the man clean across his face, she also wanted to be held close to his body again. It was frustrating and inconvenient to be truthful, but it was thrilling. Maybe Roy was right.

39

Maybe she was making a big mistake. Maybe she should have stood her ground with Wayne and told him to leave her alone. He was persistent and seemed to enjoy disrupting her and inserting himself into her life. Was this how he hooked the women? Kept at them until he wore them down like wind on a mountain peak?

Maybe, but his soft spot for kids was her weakness for him. She loved seeing Roy so excited, and she loved the way Wayne talked to the boy. She had watched him at the gala a day before. She had kept her distance, but she had watched how he appeased them, supported and encouraged them. She didn't want to admit it, but there were a handful of redeeming qualities about the man that, despite her best efforts, she couldn't overlook.

She hoped and prayed for her own sanity, that he would do something irrevocable on their upcoming date. Or, if that didn't work, she hoped he would just be bored of her so she could get back to her life. Back to things that made sense, because she knew attention from a man like Wayne was not sustainable. Even if she wanted it to be, which of course, she didn't.

| 8 | Oil & Water |

"Hey Ma," Desi said, pulling the woman into her arms. She adjusted the covers so they covered the woman's feet.

"If I wanted my toes covered, I'd have asked for it." The older woman frowned with a stubborn set on her lips.

"Mhm? Well, they felt like blocks of ice, so I'm going to beat you to the punch."

"Stop mothering me, child. I'm still your mama."

She smiled, grabbing a couple of wrappers and the empty water cup off her bedside table. "I'm sure you'd never let me forget. Where's Derrick?"

"Upstairs somewhere, I think. Always on that daggum phone."

"He's a lawyer, Ma." She went into the kitchen, discarding the garbage and filling up the cup with filtered water from the fridge.

"Must not be a good one, 'cause he's always broke."

"Ma!" She glided back into the room and set the cup on the table.

"What?" The woman laughed, her eyes lighting up. "I love the boy, you know I do, and I'm proud he went on and made something of that brain of his, but you know, same as I do, that he's not tapping into his full potential."

"He wants to use his license to help people."

41

"Well, he needs to worry over helping himself first." She pushed the button for the bed to sit up. "All that schoolin', all them damn loans, and he's drownin' in debt. To top it off, he's working for the goddamn government. Wish that boy would wake up. That's what I don't understand about your generation. It's like the hustle gene didn't get switched on..."

Desi tuned her mother out as she worked on tidying things up and opening up the windows. It was always the same conversation about Derrick. Truth was they both had education, both had jobs, and both still struggled to make ends meet and help their mom with her medical bills.

"Ma?" Desi ventured after a while of the room being quiet.

"What's on your mind, baby?"

"I-I was only able to pay some of the medical bills this month."

Her mother sighed. "It's okay. This is not your burden. You can't take on too much or you'll end up like your father."

"Ma!" She hated that her mother so carelessly mentioned her father like he was just another topic to bring up.

"Hey sis!" Derrick strolled into the room, cutting the tension like he was always able to do. He pulled Desi into a robust hug and kissed her on the cheek. "You look good, as always."

She examined her sibling. "You too." He'd been spending more time in the gym; she could tell that as he was turning his baby fat into muscle.

He smiled, showcasing a dimple. "Thanks. What's new with you?"

"What he really wants to know is, are you dating anyone?"

She frowned up her nose. "Nope, and I'm good with that."

Her mother waved her off. "No woman worth her weight in gold is okay with being a spinster. Not even me, and I'm as independent as they come. It's not natural, being on your own forever."

"I have my students and other pursuits to keep me happy. I don't need a guy to do that." And she certainly didn't need some pesky, troublemaking cowboy. It was his fault she was in this pickle. She had paid the money her mother would need and taken it out of her savings, for as long as she could. The savings wouldn't last long, though. She needed her damn clowning job back.

"Derrick, we'll need you to put in a little extra this month."

He frowned. "I thought Desi had it covered."

"Well, if she had it covered, we wouldn't need a little extra from you—"

"It's just temporary. I have some things in the works."

Derrick exhaled. "Milking a dry cow is not going to get you any milk. I'm doing all I can."

"You can stop playin' around with the damn government and get you a job in the private sector."

"My job isn't the problem."

"He's right!" Desi chimed in. "He's paying over half, I got the rest."

"But you said—"

"Don't worry about it. I-I'll just do some tutoring or something. It'll work out."

Their mother took a deep breath. "I know your brother went to school and read a lot of books. But words aren't numbers, so let me break it down. Your sister's a teacher and you're a lawyer. You have the potential to make four times what she does—"

"I'm not going to sell my soul for anyone! I'm giving it all I got—"

"Don't you dare, boy. When your daddy died, I was a single mother raisin' two babies, TWO in this shit out here. Didn't use a drop of that payoff money they tried to put on me. I gave it all I had. Paid for half your school, half of hers, kept us alive. I worked and I slaved and I worked some more."

Her brother stood with anger in his eyes. "Wait, you never used the money from dad's settlement?"

Their mother looked away, disgust in her brown eyes. "They tried to pay me." When she met their eyes again hers were moist but determined. "Pay me, like he was a used car—" Her breath choked on the words and her children were at her side immediately. "I'd work myself into the grave before I touch that money."

"Ma, what did you do with it?" Derrick wanted to know.

"Split it and gave it to a broker to invest for you two."

"All that money has been growing in the stock market all this time?" Derrick stood up and held the back of his head, his arms spread wide. "Do you know how much money is in those accounts now? You could be well taken care of, and much more."

"I don't want it," she said with determination.

"But you'd rather work us to death instead?"

"I—"

"We don't owe you anything, mom," Derrick said before the woman could get out another word. "We're using that damn money and you're going to let us." He pulled out his phone and started dialing as he strolled out of the room.

"Don't worry. I'll talk to him."

Her mother grumbled and crossed her arms over her chest before her attention drifted to the television that was muted. "Oh yes, turn that up. I usually hate commercials, but that man has a nice pair of glutes."

Desi frowned at her mother, who was turning up the volume on the television. She froze when she heard the familiar rumble of her persistent rogue's voice.

She glanced over her shoulder to see *him* walking in a field with a horse, the camera zooming in on his jeans.

She swallowed.

Will I never be rid of this man?

| 9 | Moon Dust |

"You look gorgeous." Wayne's smokey voice warmed Desi's insides.

"I know," she retorted as he closed the truck door with her in the passenger side. She sounded confident; but, truth was, she was nervous.

He jogged around the truck and hopped in starting it up.

There was silence.

"Well, aren't you gonna compliment me?"

She glanced over at him from the corner of her eye. She clenched her thighs together, taking in his fine-fitted, dark-washed jeans and a solid, black dress shirt tucked in at the belt. His straight sun-bleached hair hung just above his shoulders, shiny, presumably from a recent wash. The car smelled like tobacco, leather, and a deep sandalwood fragrance that was either his cologne or deodorant or both. She hated that it stirred her blood.

"Is that what you're waiting for? For someone to tell you that you're a dashing devil, that you're irresistible to every freaking floozy in this town?" She faced forward and took a deep breath. She glanced at him from the side of her eye when there was just silence. "Are we going or what?"

"You're just going to be difficult all night, aren't you?"

She displayed a toothless smile in his direction. "That's the plan."

The wicked man smiled so wide it made Desi shrink away from him and frown.

"Good. I ride bulls, baby. I love a challenge." With that, he put the car in drive and pulled out of the school parking lot.

Dear God, she thought. *This could be a very long dinner.*

She turned the radio on and scrolled through the stations in his big ass truck. What the hell did he need the fuel-guzzling thing for anyway? She got excited when her favorite country song blared through the surround sound speakers. She started singing the song out loud.

What the hell? If I have to be here, I may as well have fun. Might even turn the man off so he can move the hell along. When the sappy love song faded into another, she glanced over at Wayne, who had a smirk tugging at the corner of his wide mouth.

"What? Was that annoying?"

He shook his head. "Not at all, darlin'. You have a pretty voice." He switched lanes. "I have to say, I'm surprised at your song selection."

She crossed her arms over her chest. "I live in butt-fuck-nowhere. What else is there to listen to?"

"Touché." He smiled over at her.

Damn rogue.

She grimaced and looked out the window when her guts betrayed her. *God, am I just like any other stupid bimbo in this town and probably half of Texas?*

When they arrived at their destination, he hopped out of the car before she could unbuckle her belt and pulled her door open for her. He helped her out of the cab, even though she didn't need his help. She climbed pen walls and hopped into barrels. Had he forgotten? She didn't say anything when he opened the door to the restaurant, pulled out her chair, or placed a napkin in her lap. *Who the hell is this man?*

They were right outside San Antonio, near thirty minutes, forty if you drive the speed limit, which Wayne didn't, from their small town. It was a nice Italian restaurant and she was frankly surprised he had made the effort.

"I hope you like I-talian food."

"*I*talian."

He frowned. "That's what I said."

"No, you said I-talian with a long 'i' sound. It's Italian with a short 'i' sound like you'd say the country's name: *Italy.*"

He stared at her for an extended period of time before he finally spoke. "I didn't really understand a thing you said. I thought an "i" was just an "i". If you say it's Italian, though, then I believe you." He opened the menu and started looking at it.

There was a long silence during which Desi scolded herself for being a prickly jerk. She glanced up at Wayne from over the edge of her menu. Her eyes quickly darted back down when his cool grey-eyed gaze met hers. She tried to focus on the words, but all she could think about was how handsome he was. His facial hair was lined up. Well, mostly. He was still a little scruffy, but she rather liked that.

She cut her eyes his way again and started when she found him staring at her. The corner of his wide-set lips pulled up.

"What?" she wanted to know.

"I'm just going to stare at you instead of acting like I'm not. Feel free to do the same."

She rolled her eyes and propped the menu up between them, but she couldn't hide the smile on her face.

She looked into his smiling grey eyes when he tipped the menu down. "Ain't no need to hide from me, pretty Miss Limb."

She folded the menu and reached for her water, ignoring the warmth in her cheeks. She frowned when she looked across the table and saw him massaging his wrist. It was then she noticed it was wrapped.

She gasped. "What happened?"

His low laughter brought her eyes to his face.

"What's so funny?" she wanted to know with a frown twisting her brows.

He reached across the table and stroked her cheek with his thumb. "You're fuckin' gorgeous when you fret over me."

She leaned back in her chair. "I'm not fretting."

He reached across the table and took her hand in his. "Sure you are." She swallowed when his calloused thumbs rubbed the back of

47

her hand. The logical part of her was telling her to pull away, but something else was telling her she wanted those rough hands to not only hold her hand, but also trace the curves of her body. She brought her attention back to his wrist. "Seriously, what happened to your arm?"

He shrugged his eyes fell to his retracting wrists. "Tender-right-ness, or somethin' 'other."

She giggled. "Tendonitis."

"Whatever you call it, Miss Smarty Pants. It won't keep me from ridin'—" He paused when she touched the wrappings.

"All it's from is failed healing or repetitive trauma to a tendon." She cocked her head to the side and frowned, suddenly upset that the man was hurt. She was certain he was too careless, too rough with himself. "With proper care and some time, it could heal completely."

"Yes, doctor."

She looked into those moon-dust eyes for a long moment. She wondered what he saw when he looked at her. She knew he thought she was attractive, but in what way?

"Ready to order?" She started when the waiter spoke.

Wayne didn't take his eyes off her as he replied. "Yes, sir. I think we are."

| 10 | Permission |

"Who was that man?"

"Huh?" Wayne had been in his head ever since she had touched his hand at dinner. It was fuckin' with his mind, how caught up he got. Literally, his words were stolen from his mouth, and his mind. He'd been touched in far more sensitive places. When she touched him, completely harmless, his cock thickened. He kept seeing her dark eyebrows pulled together in concern. *Concern for me.* She fuckin' cared. That shit made him wanna say *yeehaw!*

"The man who came through the rodeo the day you groped me in the barrel. Certainly looked out of place with all his sweating and his clothes." She chuckled lightly to herself.

"Uh, oh, yeah. He was some guy from an advertisin' agency up in Dallas."

He met her dark eyes in the dim lighting of the car. "That right?"

"Yeah."

"What they lookin' at you for?"

He frowned at her. "Uh." *How'd she know?* "What makes you think they were even after me?"

She raised an eyebrow at him. "I may not be the most likely lover of the rodeo, but I know a thing or two."

"That right?"

She nodded. "Bet your sweet ass it is."

A silly push of joy erupted from his middle and came out of his mouth in a burst of masculine laughter. "Please, enlighten me."

"Suppose you been wanting your ego stroked all evening long."

He had something else in mind, but he'd settle for his ego.

"It's beyond your record, because, let's just be honest, Hartwood and Craimer have higher scores than you. But you do have something they don't."

"Yeah, what's that?"

"Showmanship. I don't think I've ever seen someone dismount from a bucking, angry bull quite like you. You make it look easy, like riding is just—"

Her words caught in her throat when he leaned over and smashed their faces together. They were at a red light a couple of blocks from the school, a couple of moments away from him saying goodnight. He might be jumpin' the gun, but she was talking about him. Her passion and excitement made him just... made his brain stop functioning properly and he had acted on impulse.

He pulled away waiting for the sharp sting of her hand contacting his face or her breathy proclamation of how good at kissin' he was. The former was more than he deserved, if he was bein' honest. When neither of those scenarios played out, he opened his eyes.

She crossed her arms over her chest and looked out her window. He felt the chill of her complete disengagement down to his toes.

His chest tightened and terror filled him.

Closed off.

She was shut down. Where he might have had a second date, he now only had her icy silence.

He pulled into the school parking lot, put his car into park, turned it off, hopped out and jogged to her side. The entire time he was racking his brain trying to figure out how he was going to salvage the date. This was his only shot. If he fucked it up right at the end, he'd never allow himself to live it down.

She was already pushing her door open when he grabbed it and opened it the rest of the way, helping her down. He looked around the empty parking lot and frowned.

"Where's your car?"

"I walked." She avoided his eyes, her arms still crossed.

He frowned and stuffed his hands in his pocket. It was the only way he would be able to keep his hands to himself. He wasn't used to this, holding back. He couldn't remember the last time he had had to. Women wanted him. There was no need for second-guessing. "Why would you walk?"

"Because I don't live far," she said through clenched teeth. "Why'd you do it?"

He looked up at her from his boots, trying to pull apart the jumbled-up words in his brain. "You're going to have to be more specific."

"The kiss? The unsolicited ki—" She yanked her arm from him when he reached for her.

"Desi—" he pleaded, since begging seemed his only option.

"Here I'm thinking things are going well, that maybe you can be a gentlemen—" She stopped herself with a frustrated growl, turned and started walking away.

Panic started in his chest. He jogged to catch up with her. "I-I'll give you a ride."

"I need the walk," she snapped. She kept walking, her shoulders near to her ears. Her hands were stuffed in the pockets of the jean jacket over her flowing dress. The yellow made her brown skin glow. Her unique, familiar floral scent assaulted him all evening. It was doing a number on him right there in that moment with the wind catching it and tossing it right up his nose.

"I'll walk with you."

"I'm fine! Don't need no man to save me."

He grabbed her and turned her to face him. "Ain't said nothing 'bout saving. I just want to make sure you make it home safe is all."

"You know well as I do that everyone is asleep in this speck of a town."

"You know well as I do that ain't really true." They stared at each other for a long moment until she exhaled and focused on the pretty wedge sandals on her manicured feet. He wouldn't say he was a foot person, but they were just as gorgeous as the rest of her, or at least what he had seen so far. He let his hands fall from her person missing the heat from her body.

She turned and started walking.

The fabric wrapped around her legs when the wind blew and he wished he were that damn cloth. What the hell was wrong with him? He made fun of men who thought what he was thinkin'.

She paused and glanced back at him over her shoulder. "You comin' or what?"

Joy filled his chest and he took a couple of steps to join her stride.

"It's a left up here."

They walked the remainder of the two blocks in silence. It was less than eight minutes, but he spent the entire time beating himself to death on how he had acted. But he was grateful she had given him a second chance. Allowing him to join her was more than he could have asked for.

She opened a white picket fence to a picturesque little cottage. The garden, though bathed in moonlight, was small but handsome. He could tell a lot of work and love had gone into it.

He followed her up a few stairs to the surprisingly spacious wraparound porch.

"Desiree—" He cleared his throat. "I mean, Miss Limb. I'm terribly sorry for earlier. I shouldn't have done that. I shouldn't have kissed you without your permission. It was wrong of me." He kicked the wood boards, his attention on his shoes. His hands were, again, stuffed in his pockets so as to not get him in further trouble.

After she didn't say anything, he chanced a glance up at her and paused when he saw how her pretty dark eyes were gazing at him. The light from the lamp by the door was reflected in them. The corner of her mouth was pulled up.

She moved toward him, making him stand straight. She outlined one of the buttons on his shirt with her finger. She was so close, he could smell her, feel her heat, see all the little spirals that made up her bountiful crown of curls.

She tilted her head back so their eyes met. "I accept your apology." Her eyes fell to his mouth and hers parted. His thighs tightened at his cock's reaction. Her eyelashes rested on her cheeks. She was so fuckin' pretty, it was painful.

There was a pause before her eyelashes fluttered open. "What's wrong? This is the part where you're actually supposed to kiss me."

"I'm gonna wait."

She frowned. "For what?"

"Permission."

A bright smile pulled at her high cheekbones, pronouncing them. She smoothed her hands up his chest and linked her arms around his neck.

"Permission granted."

His devilish hands broke free of his jeans' pockets and easily found her slender waist. He deepened the kiss, pulling her body flush against his. Every cell in his body started to sing, understanding that particular part of the interaction. Understanding the intimacy of touch, of play, of need, of want.

He pulled away, which took willpower he wasn't sure he even had.

He tried to calm his breathing, as well as the shouts from his more manly parts. His heavy-lidded eyes finally opened then fell to her mouth, slightly pink from their intimacy. "Your lips are so soft," he whispered, stroking the bottom one with his thumb. He hadn't really intended to say that out loud.

He grabbed the keys, put the one she had isolated into the lock and opened her door. "You should go inside." He grimaced when she slid from his hands. He missed her warmth already and the feel of her soft curves against him.

She paused before closing the door and glancing out at him. "Thank you for this evening. It was... unexpected."

The corner of his mouth lifted as joy filled his chest. "My pleasure, Miss Limb."

"You can call me Desi."

He smiled from the inside out. He almost reached for her, but instead stuffed his hands in his pockets. "The Chapman's ranch has open riding Saturday mornin'. If you're not busy, I'd like to take you."

She was peeking out from the gap in the door. "I'd like that. I'd like that a lot."

"Nine in the morning. I'll pick you up."

"Eight-thirty, and I'll meet you there."

The corner of his mouth pulled up when he met her teasing brown eyes. "I thought we'd moved on from this, Desi." He liked being able to say her name.

She giggled, making him smile too. He looked off in the distance, sure he was fuckin' blushin'.

You're too old to blush, Wayne, he scolded himself.

"Fine." Her voice was sweet as honey. Made him imagine how she'd say his name when he'd have her wreathing under him. "Eight-thirty and you can pick me up, but—"

"Don't be late." He interrupted her glancing into her dark eyes. "Trust me, sweetheart, I wouldn't dare."

She smiled and whispered a goodnight before she softly closed the door.

A silly smile pulled up both sides of his mouth once he was alone on the porch with his thoughts. *Well I'll be damned Wayne you pulled it off!*

Now all he had to do was...wait.

| 11 | Breathtaking |

Wayne handed Desi the reins to the beautiful grey and black spotted mare. She rubbed her hands along the large animal's mane, fed her an apple, then stroked her nose.

"Good, pretty girl. Aren't you, Beauty?" she cooed, nuzzling her face against the horse's.

She glanced over at Wayne, who had his eyes fixed on her even though he was chatting with the ranch owner, Mr. Chapman, a handsome older man whose wife had died several years before of cancer. He didn't seem to have any interest in remarrying, despite his children's concerns. Betty was his soulmate, he'd say and that seemed to be all he had to say on the matter.

Wayne strolled up to her with his stallion in tow. "Say we ride up to Canyon State and take a trail north from there."

She smirked. "Say I race you!" She hopped up on the horse and took off out of the ranch. Her father took her horseback riding all the time when she was a young girl. When she started teaching in the small town, one of the first things she picked back up was riding. Once she met Mr. Chapman, she had no plans of going anywhere else.

She closed her eyes, feeling the wind rush past her face. She glanced over her shoulder when she heard the strong clomping of the stallion quickly gaining on them. They were neck and neck.

"What do I get when I win?" he shouted over the wind with a handsome smile on his face.

"Bragging rights."

"Oh, come on, you can do better than that." The wind whipped his hair away from his broad forehead.

She smiled, urging her horse faster. "Fine! I'll cook for you."

He raised his eyebrows in amusement. "I hope you make a mean gravy." He powered forward, taking the lead easily.

She smirked, pushing her horse to catch up. "What do I get when I win?"

"You won't." He shrugged, a cocky grin on his face.

She laughed. She couldn't help herself. It was the reason why she both liked and loathed men. Especially men like Wayne. Arrogant, self-assured, and sexy as fuck in their confidence, even if it was ill-placed. "Let's say luck shines on me."

He slowed a bit in thought. "Not sure. What do you want?"

From him? There were many things, but most she'd never tell him. His ego was big enough. "To ride a bull."

He frowned deeply and slowed his horse. "Takes a lot of training."

"I think I'm well-equipped. I'm around them all damn day at the rodeos."

"That's different. Ridin' is dangerous."

"And clowning is not?"

He frowned and slowed down the stallion. She had to slow her horse down, turn around and meet him. He met her eyes after a moment, his churning with emotions she couldn't quite place. "Now that you mention it, I'd prefer you on the safe side of the pen either way."

She ignored the heat that floated in her middle at his concern. She had thought he'd be the carefree type. She smiled to lighten the mood, and to keep her thoughts away from undressing him. He'd lifted enough skirts in his day. He didn't need to get under hers, too.

"Well, Wayne. I'm taking that worried look as you accepting defeat. If you cross that line before me, there's nothing to worry over, is there?" She turned and took off toward the State Park. He went flying past her like the devil hell bent on a mission. She veered off, taking a shortcut Mr. Chapman took her through the woods.

She laughed in her head.

Men, always with the brute force.

True, her mare was slower than his horse, but distance from her point "A" rather than from his to the point "B" was substantially shorter.

She pounded down the dirt path, the horse's labored breaths telling her to slow down. She calmed to a casual pace and rubbed the horse's mane.

"Not as young as you used to be, aye girl? Me neither. I get it." She hopped off the horse and grabbed her reins when they rejoined the main path.

Several minutes later, Wayne and his horse stormed up to them in a rush of wind and pounding hooves. He slowed and came to a steady walk next to them.

"Wow! That's some good sportsmanship. You're just going to, what, walk your horse across the line to prove how clever you are?"

She stared up at him. "You won."

He frowned and gazed down at her for a moment before he dismounted. "What do you mean?"

"Beauty is tired. I pushed her too hard. You won."

He hopped down off his horse with all the grace and skill of a man born to ride. He walked next to her in silence for a few paces.

After a while of them walking, each in their own head, he nudged her. "So, what you cookin' for me, Desi?"

She smiled over at him. "Oh, you know, the standard stuff. Beet salad with wheat germ on rye."

She laughed out loud when he recoiled with a look of distaste on his face. "Sounds … um … different."

"I'm joking. I guess I'll have to pull out my grammie's old recipe book."

A wide smile spread across his face, making his eyes twinkle. "Now that alone right there sounds like I'm gonna have to loosen up my belt 'fore the end of it." He stopped walking, released the reins and turned to face her. She did the same, her eyebrows pulled together, wondering what the man was thinking.

He slid a hand around her waist, pulling her closer before he cupped her cheek. "I just want you safe."

The corner of her mouth lifted. "I feel safe now."

He took a deep inhale, gazing down at her like she was something precious. His gaze fell to her mouth and he leaned down slowly and pressed their mouths together gently. He lingered there for a moment, and the gentleness of it made her feel like super-heated rubber. She leaned against him, using him to sturdy herself. He pulled away, stroking her cheek steadily with his thumb.

"Here, I want to show you somethin'." He picked her up and set her on the back of his horse, mounted in front of her and started walking up the mountain pass, holding her horse's reins while she held him around the middle.

She enjoyed having the ability to look around and enjoy the scenery without having to worry too much about where they were going or how they were getting there. After a bit they got a rock plateau. He walked the horse to the edge of the plateau. The view stole her breath.

He got down and helped her do the same. They walked to the cliff hand in hand.

"Oh my God." Mr. Chapman never took her up that way before.

"Yes, ma'am, God indeed. Ain't this the prettiest scene?"

She nodded. "It's breathtaking."

"You're breathtaking, pretty Miss Limb."

She felt the heat rush to her brown cheeks before she met his liquid grey eyes. He pulled her into his side.

"I'm finding it hard to not touch you in some way today. I hope you're not offended."

She looked up at him with a smirk on her face before she said, "Oh, if I were, you would know about it."

She smiled when laughter consumed his face and the rumble echoed in the silent air. "I want to take you to that valley someday soon." He said pointing out in the distance. "'Specially once things get to bloomin'. Would you like that?"

She nodded. "I think I'd like it a lot, in fact."

| 12 | Rough & Tough |

Desi tapped her foot impatiently as she checked her watch. It wasn't that Aubrey was late. It was that, for some reason, she was feeling especially impatient and irritable. The only thing she could think of that had caused the change was her time with Wayne. He was all-consuming. He had this presence about him that, despite her most valiant efforts to dislike him, she felt alive when she was with him, free to do what she pleased, free to go where she wanted. It was absurd, really, and if he were any other persistent man, she'd have long let him go.

"Hey Desi!"

She snapped out of her thoughts when Aubrey jogged up to her and gave her a quick hug. "You been waiting long?" The woman caught her breath and presented a smile.

Desi shook her head. "Only a few minutes. I like to be a little early." She handed Aubrey her ticket.

While they walked, Aubrey examined the tickets. "Oooo, good seats."

"Right? Pays to know a person who knows a person." Desi bumped her hip into Aubrey's as they laughed and made their way into the stadium. The roaring of oversized trucks, a busy crowd, and smell of hotdogs, nachos, and beer filled her senses. She wasn't sure why the dense stimulus of events like this did something to her. It felt like the rodeo for some reason, gritty, dirty, and exciting.

"Concessions?"

Desi frowned up at her friend. "How is that even a question?"

The other woman laughed. "If I'd have known how into these things you were, I would have suggested it a long time ago." The women headed into the arena to claim their seats.

"How's your mom?"

Desi felt the sting of the question and the weight of the answer, but she nodded instead of saying the real truth. She knew the woman was just being polite asking and she didn't mean any harm. Nobody really cared to know the truth. Besides, what would the burden really do besides get Desi sympathy that she didn't want. "She's doing well. You know, a fireball as usual." That was at least true.

Aubrey giggled. "That's a good thing, right?"

"I think so. How's your brother's first semester at college?" Topic swing.

She shrugged. "He says okay, but it's not like he'd actually tell me the truth if it wasn't."

Desi nodded. "Yeah, I'd blame it on the age gap. When he's older he'll appreciate you more."

"Yeah, soon as pigs fly." The woman laughed as they found their seats and parked their things on the chairs. "What do you want? I'll grab food since you got the tickets," Aubrey said, straightening her hair.

Desi chuckled. "You might live to regret that offer."

She settled into her seat. Her attention was on the large wheeled trucks as they sped around the dirt arena, rolling over large mounds of dirt and racing each other. The event hadn't started yet, they were just doing some pre-show stuff to keep the crowd energetic.

Perhaps she liked the event for the same reason she enjoyed clowning. She would never admit out loud that she actually found clowning fun. It was the danger, the excitement, the play with abilities that she didn't get to use in her every day.

For some reason, her mind drifted to the time she and Wayne had spent together the previous weekend. It was peaceful and rather stimulating bantering with Wayne and she liked the concern he showed her. She couldn't shake his obvious distaste for her side gig, though. Truthfully, it was no worry of his.

Her stomach squeezed thinking about the view he had showed her after their race. The way he touched her, looked at her as if she were just as remarkable as the landscape surrounding them. Her insides seemed to teem like a river whenever he was near, even if it was only in his thoughts.

As much as she might have wanted to leave him in some obscure place in her life, he had made it near impossible to think of anything except him. It was amazing how quickly he had come sweeping into her world, making it hard, then making it somehow full and exciting without having to be in a pen with an angry bull or roaring monster trucks to do so.

She cocked her head to the side. He was kind of like a bull or a Monster Truck, if she gave it some thought. She smiled at that thought.

Aubrey collapsed in the seat next to her gave an exasperated huff, bringing Desi from her thoughts.

"Thought it would take you longer than that." Desi took her hot dog, nachos, soda, and sour candies from the other woman.

"Yeah, well, when someone lets you cut them in line because he wants an excuse to stare at your ass, you act clueless." She shrugged. "Then you take the opportunity with pleasant disgust."

Desi laughed. "He didn't follow you back to our seats, did he?"

"Come on now. I thought you'd know I was better than that!"

"My girl!" Desi cheered with their large slurpees and leaned into her friend before taking a sip of her drink.

"You know I'm not one prone to gossip."

Desi's insides tightened because she already knew where this talk was about to go. "Mhm, then why do I have a feeling this is about to be an annoying conversation."

"I'm not prone to gossip, but I can't ignore video evidence. It's a simple question. Are you dating the infamous, eternal bachelor who the city loves as if he's everyone's cousin, Wayne Dunbar—"

"Ladies and gentlemen." The announcer took the spotlight in the middle of the ring, clear of trucks for the moment.

Desi exhaled, feeling the relief of avoiding a conversation she'd been expertly dodging since her first date with Wayne at the end of the previous week. She would say it was none of anyone's business, but she knew that meant little living in a small town.

| 13 | Cookies 'n Cream |

"Thank you for appeasing my craving." Aubrey said as they walked into the ice shop. "You know, training for this triathlon they don't let you have any fun. But today is my cheat day!"

Desi suppressed a yawn and smiled. "Can't say I don't have a weakness for—"

"Well, as I live and breathe."

She rolled her eyes and crossed her arms to maintain control over her body on the outside, because only the Lord knew what was going on inside of her when the man's rusty, deep voice found its place in her mind.

"Wayne Du—"

"Shh, don't finish that," the man said to Aubrey, leaning in to whisper. He looked around skeptically. "Just tryin' to have a quiet night out with my guys."

Desi grumbled. "Don't you just hate when people interrupt your reverie?" She had been tired moments ago as they left the monster truck rally, but the new energy flowing through her body made her feel wide awake.

The corner of the rogue's mouth lifted. "I don't mind some people disturbing my solace."

"Hey man!" A flushed, stocky man with short, fair hair clapped Wayne on the shoulder with a robust laugh. "It's your turn!" After him, three other men came in. One had a subdued look on his face, but amusement showed in his light brown eyes. The other two were singing some song loud and incoherently.

"And there goes the neighborhood," Desi grumbled, eliciting a giggle from her friend.

The stocky man sobered a bit. His startling blue eyes found Desi and Aubrey, looking at them as if they were bulls that had come charging into a tea party.

"Here I thought you were a friend, Dunbar. Holding out on us, I see. How rude of you to not make introductions."

Desi laughed, more in her head, and found her feet, seeing Wayne irritated for the first time. Usually he had this roguish smirk on his face. Always humorous, he was usually the one causing the mischief. "Or you're too far up your own ass to give me a chance."

"Well," the man said, straightening up and slapping the other on the chest to silence their banter. "No time like the present."

"This here's my Desi."

She frowned and brought her attention to the man next to Wayne. "Desiree Limb." The man took her outstretched hand. "You can call me Desi."

"What the hell!? Right off the bat?" Wayne protested with a hostile glare on his face.

The other man laughed. "Guess that makes me special, huh."

"This is my friend and colleague, Aubrey Mankline," Desi said, ignoring Wayne's pouts.

Aubrey blushed when the stocky man kissed her hand with a look of intent in his eyes.

"Nice to meet both you ladies. Why don't you join us for a little ice cream social?" The other two men stifled laughter.

"We were actually about to—"

"We'd love to." Aubrey talked over Desi and presented a full smile to the man.

"Guess I'll get sundaes for the table to share," Desi mumbled, forgoing hope of getting home to get under her nice warm blankets.

She glanced over at Wayne who stood next to her at the counter. "Why the hell are a band of drunk miscreants at a family-friendly ice cream parlor?"

The man let a pause settle for a moment before he smirked over at her. "I confess it's my fault. I had a hankerin' for somethin' sweet."

She rolled her eyes but could not ignore the tightening of her stomach or her increased heartbeat at the intent in his eyes.

"You're a curious woman, Miss Limb."

She looked over at him after he had ordered and they were waiting for the sundaes to be made.

"To you, I'm sure I am."

"Why the hell did you make me go through the ringer to use your first name?"

She frowned over at him, struggling to decipher what was brewing behind his eyes. He obviously hadn't gotten over the introduction thing. "Respect." She was calm on the outside, trying to appear unmoved by his rising frustration.

"Respect!" She could have sworn a puff of air came out of his nostrils. "I do respect you."

"I know." She worked with young children. She knew how to stay calm under someone else's frustrations. "Because you had to earn it."

He frowned. "The hell does that mean?"

"It's actually a simple principle, Wayne." She turned toward him, making him look at her. His eyes combed over her face and his anger was slowly melting into something else.

She swallowed and looked away, trying to maintain her focus. It was difficult, she hated to admit. "You're the type of man who has things handed to him. That's why you thought it was okay to interrupt my life and seek me out at work, mess up my clowning gig, and kiss me unsolicited in your truck."

He noticeably grimaced. "I said I was sorry 'bout them things."

"I know," she said, stepping up to the counter when they placed the sundaes on the tray.

"I got it," he said in a low voice near her ear, setting money in the counter. She glanced over at him, catching his handsome eyes.

"I'm not bringing it up to throw it in your face. What I am trying to do is make a point. If you don't earn something, you don't appreciate it, you don't respect it."

"Why'd he not have to earn your name and I did?"

"Because," she said, glancing over at him as he carried the tray to the group waiting at the table. "I don't care much if I see him again."

He retracted with a furrowed brow, noticeably thrown off. He kept her eyes locked with his and he studied her face.

"Took you long enough," one of Wayne's friends said, passing out spoons to everyone as they approached the booth with the treats.

"Aubrey was tellin' us they were at the Monster Truck rally tonight."

Wayne raised his eyebrows with a nod. "That right?"

The stocky man nodded. "Pissed I didn't go now. Was thinkin' about it."

The entire time they ate the ice cream she could feel Wayne's gaze on her intermittently. Eventually, the other two guys left to go to the bar down the street, as if they needed any more spirits, and Aubrey said goodbye to take a walk with Wayne's stocky friend.

"Guess that just leaves the two of us. I can take you home." He stood, taking the tray stacked with garbage.

"I don't live far. I'll walk."

"Let me walk you." He dumped the trays and jogged to get the door for her.

"You don't have to." She felt the heat fill her cheeks and she was grateful for her melanin. The man didn't need to know his effect on her.

"Oh darlin'. When will you understand that I want to?"

| 14 | Curious Woman |

Wayne and Desi walked in companionable silence for a while. It was peaceful, a welcome treat to all the banter back at the ice cream parlor.

She cleared her throat. "I heard you were going to be in a suit and tie in a few weeks."

He glanced over at her with a raised eyebrow. "You heard that, huh?"

She giggled. "It's a small town. You can barely pass gas without the entire town knowin' about it."

He laughed, a look of surprise on his face. "Yet you managed to elude me for quite some time."

She shrugged. "Not long enough apparently, because you didn't give up."

He let out a sound of amusement. "One day you'll thank me for that."

"Ha! You think so?" She stuffed her hands in her jean pockets.

"I know so. Now, back to that fancy to do, since you brought it up. I didn't get a chance at the red-carpet thing at the school to ask you to join me."

She frowned over at him. "I-I think Jen's more suited to do stuff like that." She laughed uncomfortably, imagining the disaster that could ensue. "Champagne is not really my thing."

He chuckled. "It'd be nice to have someone that can appreciate mud and a peaceful horseback ride. Seems like lately I'm the only one of my kind in the places I go."

She frowned. *One of his kind?* For some reason his vulnerability pulled at her. She nudged him with her hip. "Don't think the world could handle any more of ya."

"It's what I heard." He presented a roguish smirk before finding his boots. "You don't have to tell me now if you don—"

"I'll do it."

The man frowned and looked over at her as if he hadn't heard what she said. She found her feet becoming unsteady the longer they held eye contact. He was so handsome she just wanted to—

Wayne pulled her into his side and she let him, quite liking that place under his arm. It felt warm and familiar.

She rested her head on him and felt the rumble of laughter in his chest.

She frowned up at him. "What's so funny?"

"You."

She pulled away, but he didn't let her go far. "Me?"

"Yep."

She ignored her swooning innards at the way his eyes sparkled when he gazed down at her. He pulled her back to his side and kissed the top of her head.

"You're a curious one, Desiree Limb. Once you see what I see, I can finally give you everything you want."

She made a guttural noise in the back of her throat. "You think you know what I want."

"Of course. You ain't much different from any other human on this planet."

"Well, enlighten me." This ought to be good.

"You just want to be seen like we all do." He pushed open the small gate in front of her house and let her walk through it first.

"And here I thought you were some brainless, bull-riding hooligan."

The man laughed but said nothing in response.

She walked up the short flight of stairs to the porch, her mind churning with what he had said. For a long time she had thought nobody could understand her. The woman who was demure and taught elementary school kids. Who was the same woman who loved the thrill of being a clown in the rodeo. The danger, the sport, the applause. Double life? Maybe. Whatever it was, Wayne knew about it. Yet, he kept on coming back.

Aubrey didn't even know, and Desi considered the woman a good friend. Hell, her brother didn't even know and she knew the man her entire life. He had thought she was getting her money from tutoring gigs. She wasn't entirely sure why it was a secret. Maybe she didn't want to give anyone the chance to tell her she couldn't do it. Or they would do like Wayne did on their horse ride the other day. She didn't make mention to him or herself that his disapproval bothered her to some degree. She just kind of wanted to pretend it didn't exist. But someone was bound to say what Wayne did, that clowning was too dangerous.

Despite all that, she rather enjoyed spending time with him. Under his aggressive, and at times annoying, pursuit of her time and attention, he was the laid back, cool-natured country boy that she'd imagined. If, of course, she spent time imagining what Wayne Dunbar would be like outside of his tv commercials and interviews.

Once on the porch, she turned to face the man. She inhaled trying to ease the gittering of her insides. She didn't know what to do, feeling quite conflicted even in her own certainty whether to invite him in. She cleared her throat and stared at her mud-spattered boots for a long moment before finding his steady gaze from under her lashes. "I'd invite you in, but I don't want you thinkin' we're gonna have sex."

The man looked shocked before he started laughing from the depths of his soul for longer than she'd expected.

"Pretty Miss Limb, when I make love to you, it's going to be in the grass with the sun shining on your pretty face and the wind blowing through your hair."

She choked on a laugh of her own. "I couldn't see me doing something so intimate outdoors."

"Oh darlin', cause you ain't been there with me. Only thing better than the sweet outdoors is the taste of your lips, the feel of your skin under my hands," He climbed the few steps to stand before her. "Sweetest sound'll be your moaning whimper when you finally submit to me." When he slid a hand to clasp the nape of her neck, she took in a breath, trying to contain the climbing heated movement of her insides. Just his nearness was making her feel like she might come out of her skin.

She had to break eye contact with him to blush. The heat wrapped around her stomach, making her shift in her boots. She should have called him out for being so presumptuous, for being so forward. He was over-bidding his hand. It didn't go unnoticed that he said "when" not "if". As much as she might have wanted to, she couldn't ignore the glimmer of truth.

He slipped his other hand around her waist and pulled her close then rested his forehead on hers. "What're you doin' next Saturday?"

She barely recognized the airy quality of her voice. "Working."

"Sunday?"

She shrugged. She couldn't think of anything but the heat seeping from his body, through the layer of their clothes and into hers, the unsteady rolling of her guts, the anticipation that made her clinch her thighs. It seemed her body was taking on a life of its own. "No plans yet. Why?" She glanced up at him from under her lashes.

"You've got plans now."

She giggled when he pressed her against him, his fingers forming to her lower back. "Plans doin' what?"

The corner of his mouth lifted. "That you'll have to wait and see."

She looked up at him from under her lashes and raised an eyebrow. "What is up your sleeve?"

"Ain't nothin' but my arm." There was a pause after she felt the rumble of amusement in his chest. She wore a smile of her own because she didn't believe the man for one moment. She was rustling with anticipation. "I'll see you soon, Desi," he said before he leaned down and placed a sweet kiss on her lips.

| 15 | No Risk, No Worry |

The air was thick, heavy with anticipation as all eyes focused on Wayne. He slowly paged through the document as if he were analyzing the offer further. He already had made up his mind which ones he would go for and which ones were out of the question. Their counter-offer looked good. Grandma did know best. He had gotten almost twice what they were originally trying to sell him, which wasn't bad either.

He rubbed his chin and mustered a "Hmmm," before he frowned.

"Well, Mr. Dunbar, what do you think?" Liz, the fierce blond woman, adjusted her perch in the chair across the table from him. "We made the adjustments per your request, and made amendments to the compensation. So do we have an agreement?"

Wayne let the silence settle between them for a minute before passing the document to Kyle. The man put on his glasses and opened the folder, following Wayne's direction. He leaned into Wayne and whispered nothing in particular, which Wayne nodded to. "I think an additional fifteen percent on the back-end ought to bring us to an accord."

The woman smiled, presenting a confirming nod to her lawyer who made the note. "Excellent, Mr. Dunbar. I will have Cindy make the update and send it over right away."

Everyone stood. Wayne proceeded to shake the woman's hand and she leaned toward him. "This is going to be a great partnership."

"I agree."

"I'll have Clive send over the concepts and scripts for you to look over. I'm thinking in a few weeks we'll be filming all the commercials at once. It'll be a long few days, but that always works out the best in the end. How long you plan on staying in Dallas?"

Wayne shrugged. "Honestly, I'll prolly be gone before the night settles in good. Truth is, I really just love the fresh air and the sweet smell of cow manure." He laughed out loud at the city folk's curved lips and turned up noses.

"Well, before you get back home, I'd recommend the Stump & Hollow if you're looking for a good steak." She winked and hurried out the door in her stiletto heels.

She clearly knew the way to a country man's heart was a perfectly prepared piece of meat, preferably red meat with good marbling.

He wondered if his pretty woman back home could do some damage in the kitchen. He bet she could. Truth was, if she prepared an old leather shoe for supper, he'd still eat it with a smile on his face.

He pressed a hand on Kyle's chest when they walked out the full-height glass windows to the skyscraper. "Before we go to the steak place, I want to get something for Desi. I've never really been any good at gift givin' and I don't want to fuck this up."

"Mhm, okay." Kyle said pushing up the glasses on his face. "Well, what sort of stuff does she like?"

Wayne looked at the man with eyes the size of saucers. "I-I don't really know. I-I mean…"

Wayne recognized humor in Kyle's voice when he responded. "You must really like this girl, huh? Don't think I've ever seen you like this."

Wayne grumbled and headed toward the large concrete steps that led from the outdoor plaza of the building to the city sidewalks. "You think it's stupid, huh?"

The corner of the man's mouth lifted. "Not even a little. It's good for a guy like you to have another side."

Wayne stopped abruptly capturing the other man's attention. "Guy like me? Ain't no other guy like me."

Kyle hung an arm over Wayne's shoulder and kept walking down the noisy city streets. "Sorry to break it to you, but there are a million guys like you. The only difference is, you have me."

Wayne scoffed, but he liked seeing this side of Kyle, who was usually so serious. It was interesting what vulnerability and love brought out in people. He pushed the man's arm off his shoulders. "Do you have any good ideas or what?"

"Of course I do. Diamonds are always welcome. I'd be hard pressed to find a woman that frowned her nose up at diamonds."

Wayne frowned. The man didn't know Wayne's Desi. "Diamonds?" He hadn't even thought about that. "Are you sure? She's kind of country like me."

Kyle tossed a judgmental glance his way. "You asked me for my opinion—" The man broke off and turned toward the window display to a shop. "It's about the thought behind the diamond. Here, let's look in here." They went inside, the air changing. Different from the heavy dense city air, it was crisp and clean air, almost too cool.

"What can I help you gentlemen with?"

"A diamond," Wayne said, feeling rather underdressed compared to the man who approached them in a three-piece suit and tie.

"Right, well, this is a jewelry store. There are plenty of diamonds here. Are you two looking for an engagement ring?"

Wayne jerked his nose up looking at Kyle. "Naw! Something nice for my *lady*."

"Ah, right. Something nice for what occasion?"

Wayne frowned then shrugged. "Do I need an occasion?"

Kyle leaned toward him. "The man is trying to help us. Calm down." He turned his attention to the sales associate. "It's just a surprise, you're a special, wonderful person in my life kind of gift."

The man nodded once. "Well." He swanned behind the counter and pointed to a section. "I'd recommend a bracelet. Does she have nice wrists?"

"Of course! Everything on her is nice," Wayne blurted, receiving a muffled chuckle from Kyle.

"Right, naturally. Small wrists?"

Wayne nodded, rubbing the back of his neck as he approached the display.

"Then the adjustables might be the most realistic."

Wayne slumped looking down into the case. "There're so many of 'em." He mumbled. He looked until his eyes landed on one. It felt like the moment he found his beautiful, thorny little rose in that damn barrel. He didn't need anyone tellin' him it was right or wrong. He knew it was.

"That one, right there."

| 16 | Modest Offering |

"So, you and Wayne Dunbar, huh?"

Desi was startled out of her thoughts when Aubrey strolled into the break room and got her lunch out of the refrigerator. Desi finished pouring her cup of coffee, using that moment to get herself together. She needed to put on a face that wouldn't give her away how she'd been thinking about Wayne-Freaking-Dunbar in that very moment.

"Good afternoon, friend."

The woman laughed. "Caffeine drip?"

"I ate lunch a little early. This is just my afternoon cup."

"Mhm. We never got to finish our conversation at the rally this past weekend."

"Your class going on the field trip?"

Aubrey laughed before she selected a cup out the cupboard. "Yep!"

Desi nodded, adding cream and sugar to her drink. "That's good. Children should get out and learn in different environments."

"Mhm," Aubrey said, leaning on the counter near the coffee machine. "So, we're going to act like I didn't accuse you of dating the savagely, handsome reprobate who you've been swearing up and down doesn't even exist?"

Desi stirred the drink, debating on how to respond. It wasn't that she had any issues with Aubrey knowing more than the rest of the town. It was everyone else. It wasn't like they were in a private place. Anyone could be lurking.

"I think we can both agree that you nor anyone else in this town had any interest in my love life, so let's keep it that way."

"Ooh," Aubrey said, pouring herself a cup of coffee. "That was the most convoluted and political response I've ever heard. You are missing your calling. I'm starting to think you should have been a politician." The woman laughed.

"When have I ever been about putting my personal life out there for the world to see?"

The other woman nodded. "I understand. You're right and I respect that. It's just, I mean if it were anyone else dating the most eligible bachelor in town, they would be shouting to the rooftops that they had bagged the town stallion."

Desi shook her head and picked up her cup. "Nothing is bagged unless and until there's a sun-eclipsing rock on this finger, okay."

Aubrey burst into laughter as Desi walked out of the break room with a triumphant smile on her face. Truth was, marriage was so far away from her mind and with Wayne in question, not even on the docket. She couldn't imagine the man settling down, least of all with her. She was a distraction and he was a nice break from her all work, no play lifestyle that she'd been living in the past five or so years since her mom got sick.

Honestly, it was nice having a man dote on her like he—

She hesitated in the doorway to her classroom when she saw the huge bouquet of flowers sitting on her desk. She closed the door and looked around, expecting the man himself to pop out of some nook or cranny and say something in his gravelly voice that would make her panties wet instantly.

She set the coffee mug on the desk and approached the display of roses. She closed her eyes and inhaled, smelling the fragrance. It was distinct, a damp and strange smell. The rich red flowers opened up toward her as if they were offering themselves up to her scrutiny.

She let the bulb of one flower rest in her palm as she bent down to smell it deeper. The petals softly glided on her fingertips as she stroked them. They were beautiful. Had to be two dozen roses.

76

She frowned when she saw the small card tucked near the top of the vase. She plucked it from the holder, opened the envelope and smiled when she read the small white paper with text scrawled on one side in gold leaf font:

If I gave a rose for every thought of you, I'd fill up your classroom. I hope you will accept this modest token instead. Can't wait to spend this weekend with you. Wayne

Desi stuffed the note in the top drawer of her desk and nervously rearranged the flowers as the loud children filed back into the classroom after recess. She leaned on the desk, picked up her coffee mug and sipped as her students took their seats, talking excitedly about whatever had happened over their break.

One of the girls in the front, Tanya, gasped. "Oh my goodness, Miss Limb! Those flowers are so pretty." The room got quiet as the young eyes gazed at the very flamboyant floral display. "Who are they from?"

She took in a deep breath and exhaled, her eyes settled on the rather lovely roses. She cleared her throat. "Well," she ventured before setting her mug down gently on the desk, buying her time. "Though Mr. Dunbar lacks subtlety, I dare say the flowers are quite lovely. Don't you agree?"

"Wayne Dunbar?" the little girl screeched, turning to one of her friends. "I told you they were dating. My information is never faulty."

"Impossible!" Roy said with a huff, crossing his arms over his small chest and slouching in his seat. "You're not his type."

"Shut up Roy, you're so stupid. You wouldn't know anything about it. It's obvious to anyone with half a brain that he's so into her." Tanya showed something on her phone to her friends, who cooed over it.

"Put the phone—"

The boy grunted. "You're a brainless ninny you are. Life ain't no damn country love song. Men like Wayne are bold and courageous. Ain't got no time to send sappy things like flowers to some schoolteacher. Sure he's got more important things to do. Prolly sent the flowers to herself."

"Well," Desi said, cradling a bulb in her hand, leaning down and smelling it. "If I treat myself so well, what in the world do I need a man for? I should certainly spoil myself like this more often. Now!" she said with more excitement than she was planning. "Take out your science textbooks and turn to page one hundred eighty-three."

| 17 | Blades Of Grass |

Desi leaned closer to Wayne and rested her cheek on his back before closing her eyes. She took a deep breath, the familiar country air cleansing her anxiety. The steady movement of the horse underneath her and the firm man in front of her calmed her inside out.

What did she have to worry about? The world could wait. Wayne had been out of town on business stuff and she kept herself busy back home, but she missed the impossible man.

It was strange, actually. A few weeks ago, she would have laughed in someone's face if they'd have told her she'd miss Wayne Dunbar, alpha asshole number one. There was, however, a gentleness that showed alongside the rough, roguish bull rider. To her surprise, she rather liked the dichotomy, the duality, the mix and blend.

She did at times feel like her adventurous side was suppressed the more she found comfort and peace in him. Giving up control, even in small ways like allowing him to, sight unseen, plan their day, was hard for her. She didn't realize it was so difficult until the moment he stopped responding to her questions about what the plans were for the day when he picked her up.

She started from her mental drift when she felt his hand cover her arms, which were wrapped around him. It was temperate weather, warm with a calm pleasant breeze. Just enough to keep you grateful, but not enough to make you cold. She snuggled closer to him, smiling when she heard a laugh rumble though his solid form.

When the horse stopped, she opened her eyes and leaned away from him. She exhaled, taking in the scene below them. They were stopped on the top of the hill, looking down into a lush green valley.

Wayne glanced back at her over his shoulder. "Beautiful, ain't it?"

She smiled. "It is."

"Even so," he said with a pause that made her look up into his eyes. "Still think I got the better view."

She rolled her eyes, but felt the heat push up her cheeks. She was grateful often around him to have her dark skin. She swore he did it just to see her look like some silly schoolgirl with a crush. "You already picked me up, you can let the bad pickup lines live in silence."

The man laughed. "Don't be mad at the truth." She found his steady gaze under her lashes and shook her head, looking out at the landscape. It was early afternoon and the sun was bright, leaving the brilliance of nothing to chance.

The horse made his way down into the valley, the long grass brushing the top of his strong legs until they came to a clearing.

He stopped the horse, climbing down with practiced ease and turned to help her down. She could have easily gotten down by herself, but she was wearing a flowing yellow dress and gold jewelry with her coiled hair pulled into an elegant bun on top of her head. She was well aware of the role she was playing that afternoon, so she let him take her around the waist and hold her in his arms even after her feet felt solid ground.

He stroked her jaw and cupped her cheek before clasping the back of her neck. His eyes searched her face as if it were the last time he'd ever see her and he was trying to remember every detail about her.

The intensity made her insides swim and heat settled between her legs. His presence was heavy, masculine, magnetic and she loved it.

"You're just too goddamn beautiful, Desi."

The corner of her mouth lifted. "Thank you." She let the moment hover for another second, basking in his adoration. "I received your rather ostentatious display of affection yesterday afternoon."

Her presented a roguish smile. "I didn't want to make the mistake of bringing you one rose again. It's tricky because the colors mean so many things and the last thing I wanted you to think was that you were in any capacity on less than all of my mind pretty much every moment of the day that I'm not with you."

"Wayne—"

"That's why you're going to take me to meet your mama."

The shock was evident on her face. "Oh, is that what you think?" She wasn't sure why anything the man said was a shock to her anymore.

"Yes, Miss Limb. I want to meet her. I want to know that part of you."

She frowned down at his chest. "She - she's not well. I-I don't know if that's such a good idea."

"Why not? We're together, the entire town knows it."

"Y-yeah, but—"

"But?" He took a deep breath, his eyebrows pulled together. "But you don't think I'm gonna last long, huh? Can't tell if you wish I was playin' or if you just think it. But I'm not going anywhere."

"People don't ever think they're going anywhere until they're gone."

He pulled away, thoughts churning in his head even though he said nothing. He grabbed the wicker picnic basket on the back of the horse and grabbed her hand before walking them out to the middle of the clearing. He laid out the blanket and took her hand to help her remove her shoes before she stepped onto the blanket. She set neatly on the soft surface and watched him set out the meal. He poured her a glass of white wine and offered it to her with a crooked smile.

She lazed on the blanket and closed her eyes, holding the glass a moment in her lap as she basked in the heat from the sun, enjoying the breeze on her skin. She sipped the drink with a smile. When she opened her eyes, Wayne was staring at her, completely frozen, enraptured.

Her lips spread into a smile, showcasing the sparkle in the depths of them. "I know that look."

The corner of his mouth tweaked. "Good, then it will come to no surprise when you're in my arms with my lips on yours."

She giggled but her humor sobered as her mind processed his request to meet her mother. "Okay, I'll take you to meet my mother, but here's a fair warning. The woman is a pistol."

He laughed. "I could have told you that."

She scrunched her face up at him. "If you think I'm difficult, you have no idea. Ooh." Her attention was drawn to the food before her. "How did you know I loved chocolate-covered dried cranberries?" She plucked one from the open container and popped it in her mouth. "The tart, the chocolate, the sweet … oh, it's just perfect."

"I didn't know," he said, looking down at the sandwich in his hands. "I just love 'em myself."

She logged that bit of information away in her mind before she cleared her throat. "How was your trip to Dallas?"

He shrugged. "I'm not really one for city life, but it was fruitful. Came to terms with the marketing agency about the contract. I'll be pretty busy with all that hullabaloo soon."

She nodded.

"Speaking of." He pushed up on all fours and crawled to where he kept a bag of stuff and dug something out, then made his way to her. He kneeled before her, making her sit up straight. Her chest constricted when he presented a square wrapped in brown paper, that looked like the color of chocolate, with a pink bow on top.

"Wayne, what is this?"

He raised an eyebrow with a crooked smile. "If I tell you, that would defeat the whole point of wrappin' it." He offered it to her, so she set the glass to the side and took it from him, meeting his steady gaze from under her lashes.

She held her breath when she removed the wrapping paper to find a jewelry box underneath. "Wayne…" She knew the man was crazy, but surely it wouldn't be—

Relief washed over her when she saw the bracelet curled around the raised interior. The diamonds caught the sunlight, making them glisten and glitter. "Wayne!" She covered her mouth with one hand. "It's so beautiful. I-I—" He took the box from her and removed the bracelet, unhooking it and clasping it around her wrist.

She'd never had anything like this before, nor had she ever gotten such an extravagant gift from a man.

"Didn't realize how small your wrists were." He had her hand in his and stroked up the palm to the wrist and back down. The sensation that rolled through her body made her close her eyes to contain something. She wasn't sure what exactly. "I can get the chain reduced."

She looked up at the man from under her lashes. They stared at each other for a long moment before he cupped her cheek and pulled her toward him, pressing their lips together.

She deepened the kiss, linking her arms around his neck and pressing herself against him. His arms wrapped around her waist and he laid her on the blanket. He was over her, his mouth massaging hers, his hands drifting along the dress until his fingertips reached her ankles. He grabbed the hem of the garment and pulled it up, stroking her smooth legs on his ascent, grazed his hands over her butt, his hands sliding into her panties and cupping her buttockes. His other hand freed a nipple from the top of her dress and his lips abandoned hers to taste the sun-kissed skin.

She worked frantically on his shirt's buttons, pulled the sides of the cloth apart then unhooked his belt buckle. She unbuttoned the fly and pushed the heavy fabric of his jeans over his hips. He helped, wiggling out of the items and letting them collect somewhere off to the side of the blanket.

He pulled her panties off and let his fingers stroke the dampness between her legs. She sighed and arched toward his fingers, rolling her hips to the rhythm of his clever digits. He covered her mouth with his own as he stroked her, coaxing the sweet, swirling, jittery ascension of her pleasure.

She combed her fingers through the fine hairs at the nape of his neck.

He grabbed her hand and moved it down to the smooth firm length of his erection. She gasped into his mouth as she stroked him. He was so hot, so heavy around her. With her legs spread open shamelessly there was no question about what she wanted from him in that moment.

She pressed her palms against his chest, rolling him onto his back before she straddled him. His hands formed on top of her hips, moved up to her waist, then down where he had to move the dress to take hold of her butt. One hand abandoned a cheek to expose her other nipple and play with the hard nub.

"You're so freaking beautiful."

He looked up at her, the light from the sun making the colors in his eyes swirl in such a mesmerizing way. She stroked his smooth jawline and he closed his eyes. She rocked her hips back and forth, gliding her wet lower lips along the length of his penis.

"Mmmm," she moaned, grabbing a breast as the sensation sent waves of pleasure through her body. He had hold of her waist, guiding her movements.

"Awe shit, Desi. I want you so bad." He sat up and reached for his jeans, where he retrieved a condom and rolled it over his penis before he laid back down and pulled her down with him. His lips claimed hers. He held the back of her head, making their tongues tangle together. His free hand aligned his penis with her opening, and she pushed her hips toward his ready, straining erection.

Slowly, she eased down on him, her breath catching several times before he was fully submerged inside her. There was a moment where they just laid there, basking in the feeling of being physically connected.

She moaned and braced herself against his chest when he started thrusting his hips. Slow at first, but he picked up the pace as perspiration clung to his forehead.

"Awe shit," he said, kissing her shoulder and holding her tight against him. "You feel so damn good." He moaned with his lips against her neck. "I knew this shit was going to be so good."

He flipped her on her back and rested between her legs, gaining his breath. "Goddamn it, pretty Miss Limb," he said while trying to catch his breath. He shook his head, seeming to be concentrating for a long moment. "I've imagined you like this many times."

He stroked her face, his brilliant eyes gazing down at her. "I'd like to think I have a pretty damn good imagination." He pulled out and eased back in as if testing something. She muffled her own moan by biting her bottom lip. Her hands were aimlessly gliding up and down his sides and back. "But I couldn't have gotten this right." He leaned down and kissed her, then pulled back and looked into her eyes before leaning over and claiming her mouth.

He picked up his thrusts sending the warm licks of unsteady energy, excitement and pleasure sizzling through her body and filling her up until there was nowhere else for the energy to escape.

| 18 | Somehow Altered |

"That's a fancy ole dress," Derrick said, assessing her through the phone screen.

"Yeah," she said, turning to look at the back in the mirror. She really liked the back even though it left very little to the imagination. She couldn't even think how feminine and sexy she'd feel once her hair and make-up were done. This wasn't her usual deal, fancy dresses, or dresses of any kind really. She was more of a jeans and flannel kind of girl, much to her mother's chagrin.

She liked the comfort, and of course there were a hell of a lot of things that she could do in jeans that she couldn't even think about doing in the bright red form fitting dress she was wearing. She looked like a warning to all the fools who even considered coming close. She smiled.

A bull would have a field day with this one. A shining beacon telling him to charge right for her. She pointed her phone toward the mirror so her brother could get a better look.

"You look beautiful, Sis. This must be some event," he said, his dark eyebrows raising with intrigue.

"Yeah, it's a red carpet gala thing out in L.A.." She tried to hide her nerves. She was a small-town girl at heart. It wasn't like she was anxious, really, she just liked staying under the radar and this was not how you did that. Then again, allowing a freaking rising celebrity to court and charm you into a relationship was not how you did it either. There were good things. Like the fact that she got her groceries for free unprompted. She felt bad because the entire thing just felt so weird. She had no problem paying, but the clerk insisted.

She wasn't sure exactly what people wanted or expected from her. She was just used to things being simple, peaceful, pleasant, unless she went looking for something wild and exciting. Unless she donned her wild and free mask, which was what she called her clowning costume. She did the wild thing for a while then went back to life. It was like a superhero disguise.

It'd been a while since she had clowned. She missed it. Missed the opportunity to use the seven years of gymnastics she had cultivated as a child. Back before her father—

"Oh," her brother joked, piercing his lips together and raising his nose in the air. "A *gala*." They both laughed before he spoke again. "Who the hell is this guy?"

"I didn't mention any guy," she said quickly, trying to hide the nervous guilt she felt in her chest. She'd been with Wayne for almost a month and still hadn't given her mother or brother details.

The man laughed. "I'm your brother. You don't have to mention anything. I mean, it's common sense. What, a teacher's convention in formal attire out in L.A.? I think not. Could be wrong, but probably not."

"Crazier things have happened," she said, trying to prolong the side convo until she could figure out a way to divert the conversation.

"Mhm. So, you going to spill or keep treating me like I don't know you're trying to weasel out of answering the question? You have no poker face." Derrick laughed, finding more amusement in her discomfort than she liked.

"I've heard quite the opposite, actually." She thought back to her run in with Aubrey in the break room the day he sent the roses to her classroom.

"Not from your only blood sibling you haven't."

She exhaled, knowing he wasn't going to let it go. "Just a guy." Lie. That was a bold-faced lie that she was hoping her perceptive brother wouldn't pick up on.

"Not *just* a guy. Try again, sis," he stated without hesitation. She grumbled under her breath. Hope was not a friend of hers. "You know Mom's going to want to meet him, right?"

"Only if she behaves. Assuming, of course, there is a *him*," Desi mumbled when the seamstress came out the back to mark off the hem with pins.

"You know I can hear you little girl," her mother said in the background somewhere.

"That doesn't mean you'll listen," she countered with a smile that her brother returned.

"You hear her talking all kinds of stuff, Ma?" he said over his shoulder.

"Mhm, I hear her. Think she grown. Wait 'til she gets her little butt—" Her mother broke off to cough.

"Are you okay, Ma?"

"Fine. I'm fine, stop your fretting over me," her mother countered, coughing a couple more times.

"Dare, is she really okay?" Desi's eyebrows were pierced together with concern.

"I can still hear you," her mother said. She sounded tired, but still seemed to have the fire she'd always had.

"You heard the woman. She said she was fine." Derrick laughed. "Nice try, but you'll not divert my focus. What's his name?"

She exhaled, not really wanting to get into the whole thing. "Wayne."

"Well, certainly sounds like he wears cowboy boots and flannel." Her brother chuckled. "Why is he going to this fancy thing?"

She shrugged. "You ask a lot of questions."

"You're my baby sister," he said light-heartedly.

"Oh please. Stop with all that nonsense, we're like ten months apart." She rolled her eyes.

"I still came out first, which means I have to look out for you. Older brother prerogative and all." He poked out his chest with pride.

"Nosey brother prerogative is more like it," she mumbled. "Anyway." She didn't want to give him a chance to counter. "I have to go. The two of you will meet him soon enough. I'll forward my part of the money sometime tomorrow."

"Nice subject change. We'll talk later about this Wayne guy. I want to check him out, make sure he's not hiding dead bodies in his basement."

"Derrick."

"I'm so serious. You can't be too safe these days."

"Goodbye. Ain't nobody got time for you right now."

The man laughed, showing his white smile and handsome dark brown eyes. "Be safe, sis."

"Love you."

She didn't fight the smile that stained her face even after she ended the call. As the woman worked to note the hem of the dress, she stared at her reflection. The corner of her mouth lifted as she imagined Wayne's face when he saw her in it. Would she find shock, lust or pride on his face? She smirked at the following thought. Why pick one when she'd probably find all three?

| 19 | Clowning Around |

Desi straddled the gate and waited.

She smiled, looking around her. She loved this. The feeling, the anticipation, the excitement, the rodeo. It filled her up with a longing that she was afraid she'd never have if she gave up this thrill.

Clowning got her so close. So close she still got the rush, still got a piece of the experience. She wondered, for a while now, what it would be like. What it would feel like to be straddling the big angry animal instead.

The crowd cheered when the bucking bull and the bull rider came out of the gate with a vengeance. The man held on for a while, but eventually slid off. Desi and a handful of clowns jumped off the gate and ran into the pen to get the big beast's attention after he turned his focus on the rider.

The man scrambled to his feet and headed to the gate when the bull's attention was brought to her and her other fellow clowns. Some clowns were hyping up the audience with some silly stunts, while she and a couple others rounded up the bull until he ran off to the open gate he was meant to go into.

They were a distraction for the bull as much as they were entertainment for the crowd. It was interesting how their job was just as dangerous if not more, and yet people didn't see it that way. It was like the importance of teachers. As if everyone could do it, as if everyone had the skills to teach children. She loved what she did, it was just irritating that she couldn't just teach without needing to do more. Then again, she wouldn't have ever found clowning.

When she was face to face, eye to eye with the big creature, she saw his wild rage. Such an intensity that it was scary. She saw anger and will with purpose and focus. If she had half that, she might have become more. Her time in the army hadn't hurt, but it paled in comparison. She retreated from the pen to perch on top of the gate again.

She heard the announcer in a rapid, excited voice call out: "Ladies and gentlemen, we have an unexpected guest with us who's just stoppin' by to make your rodeo experience just a little bit richer. Take it away, Wayne!"

The corner of her mouth lifted when the familiar sound of his voice filled the stadium followed by an uproar of cheers. "As much as I love ridin', I love watchin' a good ol' rodeo. As a gesture to the fine riders and our loyal adoring fans, and on behalf of Racker's Beer & Spirits, we're giving away free beer for the next hour." The crowd erupted in cheers and many made their way to the concessions. She shook her head and while she set perched on the wall, she let her thoughts drift to Wayne Dunbar.

There was indeed something about the man that pulled her in. It went beyond his scruffy good looks or practiced charm. She touched her lips where he had branded her with his kisses that were, like the bull, fierce and filled with purpose and longing. Unlike the bull, they were laced with a sort of gentleness that was impossible to forget.

There was more though, wasn't there? Not just his kisses, but his touch, his claim on her body, her will, her thoughts. It was too much to give to one person she knew that. Especially a person like Wayne Dunbar. It was hard not to. When she was with him, she felt safe. Sure, that sounded silly coming from her because, well, she didn't feel that way with others. Especially men, not since her father had left. Not since he□ died.

She didn't want to forget about Wayne's reputation, though. It was no secret that he left a trail of bleeding hearts. She didn't care to listen if it had been his fault or theirs, thinking they could tame such a man. She had no such doe-eyed allusions. In fact, she had no desire to let him get that far. But he'd already gotten into her thoughts, and her pants. What was next?

When all this started, she said she'd never let him get anywhere close to where he was. She had told herself it was temporary, just to keep him off her back so she could get her job back. That, and the money she had promised to help with her mother.

Truth was, no matter how much of a pain in the ass Wayne Dunbar was, she kind of missed the man when he wasn't around. She had grown to like his surprises, the way he looked at her like she was a sunset, different every time, but still just as magical.

She jumped off the pen wall again when the next rider was dismounted, catching a hoof to the gut after he rolled off the back of the bucking creature.

It was kind of silly, she had to admit, getting on top of an angry animal, and provoking the rage in the creature further by trying to stay on it. Perhaps it was the idiocy as to why she and all the other rodeo-loving fans loved it to their core.

One of the clowns waved its butt at the beast, eliciting a laugh from the audience. The bull, however, was still focused on the limping rider, who was trying to dodge the bull's focused charges.

Desi smirked, pulling a red handkerchief from her pocket. It was in case of emergencies. She held one corner of the silky cloth and let the wind catch the rest of it. The audience calmed at the same time the beast's attention was finally averted to her. Like a matador, she stood with her legs together, the red cloth billowing in the wind. The bull aligned with her, kicked back its hooves, puffed smoke from its nostrils, then took off charging toward her. Right toward her, and right toward its pen as well.

She took a deep breath, waiting for the perfect time before she took several steps and dove into the barrel close by. She heard the audience cheer as the hooves of the beast thundered by her safe place. She cursed and touched her lip, which was throbbing.

Shit!

It was bleeding. She'd misjudged her speed when she jumped into the barrel and caught her lip on the edge.

She climbed out of the barrel and over the wall to tend her lip. Her insides filled with energy as she received congratulations and exaggerated accounts of her stunt on her way to the clowns' tent.

She did this for the money, true, but she kind of enjoyed the admiration as well. The stunts, the thrill, the excitement.

| 20 | All is Fair |

Wayne's chest buoyed when Desiree came out of her house. She turned and locked her door then walked down the three steps. He was leaning on his truck's passenger side door, waiting for her to come out.

Her beautiful face pulled into a smile that would have knocked him off his feet had he not had the truck for support.

She stopped a few paces from the car and clasped her hands in front of her. They stood there for a minute in the failing light just gazing at each other. His chest tightened as he took in her pretty yellow top and dark-wash jeans. Her hair was pulled up into a high, full, coiled puff. Subtle makeup and gold accessories called attention to her deep brown skin.

Damn, she was perfect.

She cleared her throat politely, looking down for a moment. "We'll miss the fair if we keep at things like this. Unless you weren't actually intending to drive me at all."

He laughed and pushed away from the truck to approach her. His hand slid around her slender waist, pulling her against him. He frowned when he noticed the cut on her upper lip.

"Desi—"

She cut him off as if she already knew what to expect from him.

"I misjudged how fast I was running before I jumped into a barrel. It's fine. It's already healing."

His eyebrows furrowed, recalling the fast beating of his heart as the great beast had charged past her. She had barely moved out of the way in time. He couldn't help his mind from conjuring up the situation and the physical manifestation of his terror caught in his throat.

"It's not a big deal," she said, running her hands from his forearms up to link around his neck. He took in a deep breath as the flood of desire washed over him. The feel of her in his arms again, her familiar floral scent, her touch, her compliance. He licked his lips and cupped her face in his palm before looking into her dark eyes, even darker in the surrounding darkness.

He let his thumb run along her bottom lip before his face descended to press a chaste kiss to her mouth.

When he pulled away her eyes were still closed for an extended moment. She opened them slowly.

He swallowed, certain the stupid smirk was still on his face before he reluctantly released her, turned and opened the truck door. He helped her into the truck, closed the door, jogged to the driver's side and got in.

He pulled off, taking her hand in his. "I saw your little stunt yesterday." He wasn't sure why his thoughts went back to the rodeo incident; maybe because it still bothered him. He had stopped in to announce a promo deal he was doing with a local beer company. He wasn't expecting to see Desi there. It sure did something to him though, the near miss. She was skilled, he knew that. He had seen her do her stunts. But it didn't stop him from worrying about her. He had felt so helpless at that moment. There was nothing he could do way up in the booth while she was in the pen, in the trenches, in danger.

"I'm pretty badass, aren't I?" She kept her gaze out the window.

He glanced over at her. "You're quick and crazy as all hell." There was a pause that set there while he debated whether to say what he wanted or not. "Can't help but think you put yourself in a lot of unnecessary danger."

"And what? Getting on top of the beast with a rope wrapped around its balls is any less crazy, any less dangerous?"

"That's different."

"How so? Please explain." She faced him with that sure look on her face like anything he said was going to fall on rocky soil.

"It's just I've been trainin' my entire life to deal with it."

She nodded. "Suppose I'm just a stupid woman who hopped in the ring without any training at all."

"Des—"

"That's what it is. Admit it. I'm a woman and you're a man. You should be able to put yourself in harm's way and I—"

"That's not what I said—"

"I should be at home barefoot in the kitchen cooking her big strong man a hearty meal." She continued over him making his blood heat to boiling.

"You're putting words in my mouth." True, but not in his head. That's what he was thinking if he were to be honest. He knew it was all sorts of things like sexist, but it was how he had been raised. He couldn't fight his own discomfort with the whole thing. "Little to do with you being a woman. It's that you're *my lady*."

"You think us having sex all of a sudden makes me your possession?"

His thoughts stopped momentarily and he looked at her with his eyebrows pulled together. "Is that when you think you became mine?"

It was her turn to look perplexed, which only made mischief twinkle in his eyes. He could tell she wanted to slap him and kiss him at the same time. That right there is what made the corner of his mouth pull up.

"Pull the car over."

"I will not."

He jerked the truck to the side of the road when the crazy woman started opening the door. She climbed out and slammed the door after herself. He scrambled out of his seat belt, opened his door and set to chasing after her.

She turned toward him abruptly, fire in her dark eyes. "You are so arrogant, so self-assured. I belong to no man, least of all you. I'm going home." She turned and started walking in the general direction of her house. It was a small town, so it wasn't so far away, but her walking home was out of the question.

Before she got far, he grabbed her arm, forcing her to face his frown. He clasped the back of her neck and took her mouth, tongue and all.

She couldn't even get the gasp past her lips. He made sure she was so overwhelmed with his taste, touch, the feel of his body against hers that she had no resistance left in her to escape him. He hadn't planned on kissing her, that wasn't even on his mind, at least he didn't think it was, but once there, he committed fully to the action. Even if she laid a strong hand across his face, which he'd be the first to admit was fair given how he handled things, he'd do it without regretting feeling her soft lips touch his.

She groaned when her back came in contact with a tree behind her. His hands were roaming her body. He pulled her breast from the top of her dressy shirt and suckled her nipple in his mouth.

"Fuck!" she groaned, pulling her fingers through his thick waves. She arched into him. Never a whisper of rejection, never a warning saying he was crossing a line. There was no line, only them, and he wanted her this way. "Wayne, I—"

He took her mouth again, grabbed her thigh and wrapped it over his hip. Since he had her for the first time, he had wanted her again, but his stupid schedule hadn't allowed him that privilege. But what had happened at the rodeo the previous night was too much for him. He needed her close.

"Mmmm," she moaned, feeling him hard and ready for her even through their jeans.

He rested his forehead on hers, catching his breath while she did the same. His hand formed over her ass. His fingers ventured to the heat between her legs. She shivered when he pressed his fingers against her warmth. Even through the jeans it was almost too much. She moaned and arched toward him.

"The moment I smelled you in that barrel, I knew I had to have you for myself. Discover you, find you, touch you, taste you. The fact that you're mine has only solidified further ever since."

She retorted with a breathy response. "I am no man's—" He pressed a finger over her pliable mouth.

"Desi." He whispered her name with such yearning he almost didn't recognize his own voice. "Let me worry over you. Let me—"

He held her eyes with such an intensity as if he wanted to put her in a trance. He emphasized his hold on her body when her squeezed her ass in his palms before he claimed her lips, this time gentle, paced, mesmerizing. He made sure to take his time. He wanted her to feel him to her core. "Mmm," she moaned again. She folded her hands in his back pockets and pulled him to her.

He moaned too and sucked in breath, then tipped her chin up to meet his eyes. He held them, brushing aside some wild curls that escaped her bun. He pinned her to the tree with his weight and held her eyes.

He pulled her bottom lip between his teeth, then pecked the corners of her mouth before placing a gentle kiss to her lips.

"Let me love you."

| 21 | Complete Clarity |

Wayne took Desi's hand when she looked over at him with frantic eyes. He leaned in and kissed her on the forehead. "No need to be nervous."

She rubbed her hands down her pretty yellow sundress. "I haven't brought a man to meet my Momma since sophomore year in college."

He frowned. "Well, w—" Before he could get the words out, the door opened and a tall slender man with Desi's eyes and skin tone pulled the door open with a wide smile. He pulled her into a robust hug.

"Derrick, this is Wayne. Wayne, this is my big brother Derrick."

The man laughed. "Big brother is a bit governmental, don't you think, Des?" He offered his hand. "Of course. I know Wayne. Who doesn't 'round here?" They shook hands. "Please, come on in."

Wayne looked around the space. It was bigger on the inside than it looked on the outside. He noticed pictures on the wall and on a table near the entrance with an assortment of knick-knacks. He smiled when he saw a photo of Desi as a child with one of her front teeth missing.

"Here, let me take that," Derrick said, taking the bag of groceries from Wayne's arms. "Mom's waiting for you two."

Wayne took Desi's hand and her dark eyes met his. She was so pretty it hurt every time he looked into those chocolate orbs. "Lead the way, beautiful."

A deep red filled her cheeks, barely noticeable had he not memorized everything about her pretty face down to the last birthmark.

She knocked on the door. "Hey, Mama."

The pretty older woman smiled as Desi came in and gave her a hug. "How you doin', baby?"

"Good, mama." She straightened up and cleared her throat. "This is Wayne, my, ah, boyfriend. Wayne, this is my mama, Eileen Limb."

Eileen was in an adjustable bed that had her sitting up. Her silver hair caught the light streaming in through the windows. "I don't do that hand shakin'. Come on in and give me a hug."

Wayne took note of the floral fragrance on the woman's clothes when he hugged her. It was different from Desi's, but similar. "Nice to meet you, Mrs. Limb."

The woman exhaled. "Good to finally see who's got this one always runnin' around with a stupid smile on her face."

"Ma!"

Wayne smirked, finding her embarrassment endearing. He wasn't sure if her family would even know about him. Desi was a very private person.

"Well, step over in front of me and let me get a good look at you."

He did as he was told, because if the formidable woman had birthed his fireball of a lady, he knew she was a force that he didn't want to have to reckon with if he didn't have to. "Well. My Desi sure knows how to pick 'em."

"Ma!"

"She ain't pick me, ma'am. I picked her."

"Hmm," the older woman said, crossing her arms. "Did you now. And why is that?"

He crossed his arms, holding the woman's intelligent gaze. "Mostly because she was causing me trouble."

Desi pushed out a forced laugh. "I think you have that flipped around, sir."

He laughed, mostly at the amusement on her face. "If you'dn't of been so stubborn, wouldn't've been no trouble at all." He adjusted his stance to lean on the wall adjacent. "You wouldn't've believed it. She stomped my foot right after I saved her."

"I wouldn't have needed saving if you'd have minded your business—"

A knock on the doorframe pulled Desi's glare from him. "Des, you helping me make lunch?" Derrick wanted to know, poking his head into the room.

"Yeah. Ma, you need anything from the kitchen?"

"No, baby. I'm fine. Think I'm gonna just talk on with Wayne while y'all handle the kitchen."

Wayne frowned, meeting the woman's dark, searching eyes. For some odd reason the phrase 'gird your loins' whispered through his mind. This woman was Desi's mother and though Desi might have gotten her mannerisms from the woman, he had a feeling from their brief introduction that the woman was far from always well-mannered.

When the other two had gone off to tackle the food situation, the woman focused her attention on him. "So, tell me, Wayne Dunbar. How many other Bessie's you ridin' ?"

He was used to keeping his composure but the pretty older woman caught him off guard. Wayne knew if she wasn't sick, she'd be a force just like her daughter.

"Excuse me, ma'am?"

A smirk marred her innocent facial features. "Might be lyin' in dis bed lookin' fragile, but you can bet your tight ass my mind is sharp as a tack. First place bull rider many times running, jean commercials, salsa commercials, truck commercials and I've heard on good authority that you're headin' toward more lucrative sponsorships."

"Ma'am?"

"All that money, fame, recognition. I'm happy for you, but I also know there are skirts chasing you. Women are no doubt tossing their panties at your feet."

Wayne shifted uncomfortably, as he hadn't been planning on ever having this conversation with the woman, least of all the first time meeting her. He didn't blame her, though. He was well aware of his reputation and he had done well to earn it. People changed though, only when they were good and ready, and he was. He didn't like her

99

implications, mostly because they held some truth. "I'd wager so. Don't take much for most of 'em to try."

The woman laughed, or at least that was the only way he knew how to interpret the sound. "Those heffas are amateurs compared to the parade of pussy heading your way."

He scratched his chin. He'd never thought in a million years he'd be talking pussy with a dame's mama. "Ma'am. Not sure what you're going for here. Since before I knew her name, Desi's been the only woman I've seen."

"It's new." She waved him off. "The puppy love thing will fade, and without a doubt you'll see all the shiny objects. I want to know how you're going to deal with that."

He frowned. "It's simple. I'm gonna just tell 'em no."

"I'm talking, trained girls. They know exactly what to say and what to do. How to make you feel at the precise moment. When you're down, when you're weak. When you're in disagreement with your lady. They know."

"Don't matter."

"Say you two get into a big fight. I'm talkin' sayin' things that hurt kinda fight. The kind where you limp away to lick your wounds, unsure if you'll come back to each other again, kind of fight."

He took a deep breath and held a strong stance, looking right into the woman's dark eyes. The same eyes his Desi had. "I might ride bulls, but I'm not one, Mrs. Limb. I see Desi and only her, not because of some daisy-eyed puppy love, but because I choose to only see her. She's the one I want."

After a long while of holding each other's eyes, the woman's serious expression broke into that of amusement. She took a deep breath and closed her eyes, leaning back into the bed. "Well, alright, Wayne. Alright. Don't be a stranger now. Come on over here and sit by me." She tapped the bed and he made his way to her side and perched there. "She's a pretty girl. Isn't she?"

"Yes, ma'am. Looks a lot like her mama."

The woman chuckled before coughing into her fist. "That's a good thing, 'cause her daddy was an ugly son of gun."

Wayne choked on air.

The woman laughed maliciously. "Ugly, my goodness, but that man worked. Worked for me, worked for his chil'ren, worked himself right into the grave, he did." She took a deep breath. "He loved. He loved so hard. Never felt that safe eva in my life."

Wayne's chest felt heavy. Desi had never told him how her father had passed. He brought his eyes back to the woman before him.

The older woman started coughing again. She reached for the glass on her bedside table and drank its contents. "Would you mind," she said between coughs. "More water, filtered, from the refrigerator, please."

"Of course." He took the glass with a nod and made his way into the kitchen. He paused a few steps from the kitchen when he heard Desi speaking in a hushed voice.

"She'll listen to you. You have to convince her to sign the paperwork so we can use the money in those accounts."

"Don't you think I already tried that? She's trying to get me to take a private sector job."

"Why won't you? If you can make more—"

"Don't you start too."

"Well, we're both tapped out. I'm doing all I can."

"You're not making the portion you agreed on. I put my loan repayment on hardship deferral, I sold my condo and moved back home! I've done all I can."

"What? Should I move back home too? Wouldn't that be cozy."

"Maybe so. You can get a job teaching at a tech school or something."

Wayne cleared his throat and strolled into the kitchen. "I'm on strict instructions to get filtered water from the 'fridge."

Desi's frown quickly pulled into a smile when she laid eyes on him. It made his chest clench that he brought her joy like that.

"Sure, I got it. Lunch's almost ready." She took the glass and pushed up on her tiptoes to kiss him before she turned and headed to the refrigerator. He didn't need to hear any more. His Desi wasn't movin' anywhere. If she needed help, why didn't she come to him? He huffed, the answer quickly coming to his mind. He knew his Desi better than most. The stubborn woman wouldn't ask for help if she needed it to save her last breath, so he'd give it to her. She didn't need to know it was him, though, 'cause she'd reject it for sure if she did.

He looked in his hands when he felt the cool glass. "Can you take this to mama?"

The corner of his mouth lifted. "Of course, honey."

"Mmm," she said, kissing him twice. "I'll let you know once everything's ready, okay?"

He nodded and slid his free hand around her waist, pulling her to him to kiss her one more time.

"Okay, okay, go before you start something." She said with a playful giggle.

"I ain't start nothin'. That was all you."

She slipped from his hold with a silly look on her face and made her way back over to her brother, who was focused on his task near the stove.

Wayne knocked on the doorframe to Eileen's room before he entered, placing the glass on her bedside table and taking a seat next to her again.

Her perceptive eyes took him in, sized him up, assessed him. He did much the same, in awe of how much his Desi looked like her.

She cleared her throat, capturing his attention. "He never stopped working for me, you hear? Wasn't about providing, because before I met him, I was making it work. I dressed to the nines, mhm, you better believe it, and I paid for it all myself."

He looked down at his hand in hers then back up to tear-rimmed eyes.

"That man worked for my *love* every single day. I knew without a shadow of a doubt if he had only one breath left in his body, he'd give it to me, if only to see me smile one last time." She nodded, then let her head rest back on the pillow and closed her eyes.

He felt a depth about that moment. A fierceness to keep his Desi safe, to love on her, to cherish her. It was exhausting convincing a woman so strong that he was worthy, but it was easy matching her intensity. That's what he wanted.

He looked up toward the door and saw a partial view to the kitchen. Desi and her brother were laughing about something as they cooked together.

The corner of his mouth lifted at the warmth in that place. She paused her activity when she caught his eyes. The corner of her mouth lifted, and she cocked her head slightly to the side.

The way she looked at him, the warmth in her eyes made his chest clench. It was clear to him at that moment that he wanted to keep that smile on her face for all his remaining days.

| 22 | Headin' Home |

"Are you okay? You've been kinda quiet."

Desi smiled, looking over at her handsome companion. "I'm good. It's just a lot for me to see her like that." She looked back out the window. "I'm used to her having so much spirit."

Wayne laughed. "I don't think she's lacking in spirit, despite what she might appear."

She laughed too. "Today was one of her better days. I'm glad you got to see her like that." She looked down at her leg when she felt the heat and weight of Wayne's hand on her knee. She covered his big rough hand with her own. The headlights of a passing car allowed her to see the difference in their skin tones and it made her smile. There were so many things that were different about her and Wayne. There was the obvious: black and white, man and woman, cowboy and schoolteacher. She laughed at the last one because she was only kind of just a schoolteacher. All those things were superficial. Not irrelevant, but just surface level.

If she were to be honest, with only herself, she would say she was a cowgirl in teacher's clothing. There was something, adrenaline, the roaring crowd, the risk of the arena that excited her.

"What are you over there thinking on?" Wayne wanted to know, looking from her to the road and back.

She shrugged. "Just life is all. Sometimes it seems so surreal."

"Now I can agree with that." There was a deep silence that filled the space between them until Wayne broke it. "Desi?"

"Hm?'

"Why'd you never tell me about your father?"

She froze in her spot. "What is there to say?" It came out harsher than she intended.

"I ain't know he passed and like he did."

"Don't matter. He's gone."

"Your mom said it never really set well with you."

She faced him with fury in her heart. He couldn't see her face 'cause it was so dark, but her eyes were welling up. It was her shaky voice, however, that gave her away. "Oh yeah, and what else were you and my mother talking about?"

"Honey, don't cry."

"I'm not." She lied. She turned her attention out the window and crossed her arms.

The car was silent. The air conditioner was white noise in the background. The radio was on so low, she'd forgotten it was on at all. Now all the background sounds were like sirens blaring in her ears, reminding her that she was there and Wayne was there. Between them was the tangy taste of tension.

"Desi, don't be all closed off." He squeezed her knee which sent electricity from the appendage to the space between her legs. She frowned at the sensation. She didn't want that right now.

He exhaled. "I didn't mean to make you upset. I just want to know him because he was obviously a big part of you, like half."

She ignored the delight in the soothing sound of his low rumbling voice.

"I don't like talking about my daddy." She wiped the stray tear that escaped the barricade of her eyelids.

"Why?" His voice was soft in the silence.

She shrugged. "Wasn't his time. He had so much more life." She stopped to swallow past the lump in her throat. "He— he was so strong, worked so hard. He didn't deserve to go the way he did."

He rubbed her knee and she enjoyed the sensation. It was comforting.

"Your mother said he worked himself to the bone. Said he didn't ask for help when he needed it."

"He was a hardworking black man in Texas. That was the only way you'd get anywhere close to providing for your family. He emphasized manners and work. A lazy child did not eat. Just ask my brother. He got cut off a few meals." She chuckled at the memory. "Daddy was right. Derrick's a lawyer now. He gets paid very well and though his love life is nonexistent, he's financially set."

"Hmm," Wayne said, mischief in his voice. "Career-focused, independent, and difficult. Why, that doesn't sound like anyone I know."

She smirked over at him. "I think, Mr. Dunbar, that you're describing yourself."

"What?"

"Mhm, running around here so focused on your career and nurturing your fandom that you'd gone over three decades without a real loving relationship."

"Difference is, when she fell into my lap, I knew it and refused to let her go." He grabbed her hand and kissed the back of it. Passing headlights caught his eyes and made her smile.

She cleared her throat when familiar heat wound its way slow and steady through her guts. "When are you filming your commercials?"

"Well, I've got the big commercials coming up here in a couple weeks, maybe. Things got moving real fast when I accepted the offer. With some amendments of my own, of course."

She laughed. "I thought it was a good offer."

"Yeah, well, like my grandmama said, 'Never take the first thing they hand to you.' I think it was mostly off principle, not so much that what they handed over won't be good. It lets them know that you ain't no one to trifle with."

"Hmm," she said, tapping her chin. "Sounds just like what I did to you."

He laughed out loud. The heavy sound made her soul sore. "That's sure right, honey. And I'm glad you did. Nothing wrong with a healthy dose of fear in a relationship."

"Fear?"

"Mhm. Fear of fuckin' up. Standin' up for yourself and what you want and don't want is sexy. Sets me right in my place."

Yep, right between my legs. She blushed at the thought.

He stopped the car and cut the engine. "We're here." She frowned, looking out the window.

"Wayne, where are we? You said you were taking me home."

"No, I said I was taking *us* home."

She frowned and looked to the side, obviously confused, because it sounded like he said what she said, but the outcome was not the same. "This is not home."

"Of course it is. This is my ranch."

Before she could get her bearings straight, Wayne was on the other side of the car pulling the door open. "It's so dark."

"Yep!" he said, leading her with ease through the darkness. "There are four steps here." She heard him unlock the door before it creaked open. He clicked on the porch light and she smiled at the screened-in space. It was alive with various plants, a large wooden swing, soft floral upholstered couches and some leaning little side tables. It looked like a little old lady might live there, not a rough, tough bull-riding cowboy. He opened the door to the house itself and led her inside, turning on lights along the way.

"Hm, not the bachelor pad I was expecting."

He laughed. "I ain't no city boy. I like comfort and for things to feel like ho—" The words got caught in his throat when she dove on him, smashing their faces together.

He was stiff and surprised for a few moments, but he quickly got on board. He pulled her into his strong arms and she wrapped her legs around his lean waist. Her body ignited in flame, in want, in desire. Maybe it didn't look like it belonged in that place, but she didn't care.

She wasn't sure where the bed was in the house, but somehow she was lying on it. Had he climbed the stairs? Was it truly a ranch? It was impossible to know, considering it was so dark. —

She groaned when his lips found her neck and his fingers slid down her panties. Her fingers were in his hair combing, grabbing. She arched toward his mouth. which had one of her nipples hostage.

She whined his name when he grabbed her hands, which were working the button on his jeans.

"Patience, my ravenous little she-devil. I will give you everything you're yearning for."

| 23 | Morning's Glory |

Wayne didn't have to open his eyes to know where he was: home. He rolled onto his back and let the morning sounds fill his ears. He cracked an eye open and saw a dainty cast of light blue wash the walls and floor of his room with dawn.

A soft grown to his side made him glance over. His insides clenched when he saw his beautiful desert flower lying next to him. He propped himself up on his elbow to get a better look at her. Even the lack of light couldn't dull her beauty. He grazed his forefinger along her soft cheek and she stirred a little bit, but then fell back into a deep sleep with her mouth slightly open. He smiled and rubbed his thumb over her bottom lip.

She groaned and turned to face away from him.

He laughed. *Even in her sleep, she's givin' me a hard time*. He pulled her nudity into the cradle of his body and wrapped his arms around her from behind.

She was right where she was supposed to be. He closed his eyes and focused on her warmth and breathing next to him.

Women weren't invited there.

He'd fuck 'em in a barn somewhere after a ride, maybe a hotel room, or their place. He had a place he rented above the bakery where he might venture, but they didn't come back to his ranch.

He had grown up in the house. It was his peace, his oasis away from the flashing lights, cameras, people who wanted something from him. When he was tending the horses or in his garden, all seemed right. Some days it was hard to tell what was real. His life on the ranch, or riding bulls and doing jean commercials.

He wondered sometimes whether his parents would be proud of him or if they'd look down their nose at his success. It wasn't like he had planned for it. It just kinda happened. He hadn't gotten into bull riding because he wanted to get famous. In fact, before him, he didn't remember any real big rodeo cowboys getting that famous. They were local legends, heroes in their own right, but nothin' like all the crazy he had experienced.

Desi moved a bit with a stretching yawn before grabbing his hand and forming his fingers over her round breast.

All thought ceased as the soft pliable flesh sounded a siren in the breaking dawn of the day. He massaged her there and soon felt her nipple harden. He pinched the little nub between thumb and forefinger.

She gasped and pressed her butt back into him.

His dazed cock didn't need any additional incentive to figure out what the hell to do.

"Mmm," she moaned, rolling her hips back against his growing interest. She hooked a leg behind his and moved his hand down her body to slide between her pussy lips.

It was his time to groan. He slipped a hand under her, grabbed a breast and pulled her up against him while he languidly massaged her clit.

"Wayne," she whined, sending a fiendish joy through his body that stretched and grew his arousal.

"What is it?" he rumbled in her ear before pulling her ear lobe between his teeth.

"I want you."

He reached behind him into the bedside table to retrieve a condom.

Then, have him she would.

*

110

The familiar sounds of home brought him slowly into the world of the conscious. It felt vaguely familiar, like déjà vu. He rolled onto his back and opened an eye before closing it quickly. It was bright outside. A sunny day, which meant it was going to me hot. He should get up—

His thoughts paused and he opened his eyes again, squinting through the bright light and looking next to him. He frowned at the empty bed. He could have sworn it wasn't a dream, though he had woken up many times before with a rock-hard cock from having the same dream.

He rubbed himself. He wasn't hard. There was no sexual strain. He sat up on his elbows and smiled when he saw a pretty yellow dress in a pile on the floor.

He exhaled, not even knowing he had been holding his breath. He raised an eyebrow before bringing his attention back to the dress. *Does that mean she's walking around his house naked?*

That got him out of bed quick. He stretched, took a pit stop to the toilet, and headed downstairs.

He smelled coffee. The consistent squeak of the porch swing brought him outside. He kept forgetting to oil that damn thing.

He smiled when he saw her swinging and sipping her coffee. She was in one of his shirts and had one foot tucked under her butt while she moved the swing back and forth with the other and look around. "There you are. Thought you ran off." He looked out at the large expanse of land, the two barns, the gated pastures, some trees in the distance.

"This place is beautiful."

He exhaled and leaned against the doorframe, looking out at his land. "I forget sometimes."

She took a sip with a nod. "We all take things for granted."

He pushed himself off the door frame and kissed the top of her head. She leaned her head back and puckered her lips. He smiled, leaned down and pressed their lips together. He pulled away with a grunt and then kissed her again. "Why'd you get out of bed?"

She smirked. "We'd be in bed 'til the sun went down if I hadn't." She sipped her drink and brought her attention out to the landscape.

He wrapped her in an embrace from behind over the back of the porch swing then kissed her on the neck. "You say that like it's a

111

bad thing." He pulled her ear between his teeth and slid a hand down her top to pinch her hard nipple.

She gasped and arched toward his clever digits. He slid his other hand into her panties. He bit his lower lip when he found her swollen sex.

"Do you gotta do that on the daggum porch?"

Wayne started when his sister's familiar voice met his ears. "God dammit, Joey Lou. Do you gotta lurk?" He retracted his appendages. "When did you get here?"

"Right after dawn. This ranch ain't gonna run itself."

"Take the day off."

"Can't. There're things that need doin.'"

He crossed his arms over his chest. "They can get done tomorrow. How rude of me. Joey Lou, this is Desi. Desi, this is my sister, Joey Lou."

"I know." Desi said, simply before taking a sip of the coffee. "You sleep quite sound, and I wanted coffee."

"Don't worry. I won't come in there while you're fuckin'."

"Joey Lou!"

The woman shrugged and adjusted her overalls. "What? That's what you're doin'. Why call it somethin' else?" She turned and made her way with buckets and an assortment of other things toward the barn in the distance.

"Ain't got no home trainin', that one."

"Kind of like her brother." Desi glanced over her shoulder at him with a rueful smile.

"You have no idea, girlie. I've been a classy gentleman with you so far." She shivered when he leaned down and whispered in her ear. "I ain't yet shown you the rough, tough cowboy."

She pulled away enough to look back at him. "You know, Wayne Dunbar." She set her coffee cup on an adjacent table. "You talk a lot, but I'm more of a show-me kinda girl."

He growled with an evil smirk and grabbed her up over the back of the chair, tossing her onto his shoulder. She let out a startled squeal and giggled as he carried her into the house.

If she was going to tease the bull, she was going to catch the horns.

| 24 | Silly Infatuation |

Wayne unwrapped his hand and flexed it with a smile. It was feeling better with Desi's balm and massages. He'd been doing less ridin' too. He supposed all the marketing hoopla had come at a good time, because it was a good excuse for him to miss out on what he loved. Missing out, however, meant he'd look an ass when it was time to perform, which was what had just happened.

He looked up with a frown when a whiff of a familiar scent found his olfactory senses. He saw his sexy little rodeo clown leaning on the opening to the barn.

"How long you been standing there?"

"Long enough." She pushed off the frame and strolled leisurely toward him. He licked his lips, knowing under the baggy clown costume were delicious curves wrapped under smooth skin.

She combed her slender fingers through his hair and massaged his scalp before pressing a kiss to his temple. He exhaled and leaned back against a bale of hay.

"Thank you," she whispered in his ear. It was the emotion behind the words that made him open his eyes. Her big brown eyes were moist.

"For what?"

"For what you did for my mom. She was able to see the specialist and they have her on new medication. Things are looking up." She inhaled and her voice was shaky, but the tears stayed on the edge of her eyelids. "Things were so behind. She almost lost her healthcare benefits because we were struggling to pay the premiums."

He exhaled and brought his attention to his wrist. "I told Kyle to contribute anonymously."

She laughed. "He did." She took his hand and started massaging it in the gentle way she did. "But I'm not stupid. I tell you about my mom and a few days later her bills are paid. Coincidence?"

"Miracle?" He shrugged. "God does work in mysterious ways." When she stood, rubbing his thighs, he opened his legs to let her stand between them. Under the clown makeup, he couldn't make out any of her features except her pretty, deep-brown eyes.

"My grandma might agree with that, but she also said he worked through people." She linked her arms around his neck and her intoxicating scent wafted up his nose.

He inhaled and relaxed as she leaned into him. "You missed me out there. I did a round off into a barrel. Seemed to be a crowd pleaser."

He smiled when she started scratching the scruff under his chin. "A really smart teacher once said, 'A smart rider would run to safety and let the rodeo clowns take on the beast.'" Her laughter made his chest sore.

"You never listened to her before, so why start now? It's not like I'd actually want you to stay in the pen. Just, you know, linger a bit in safety and watch me show off a little." He laughed, but it didn't reach down to his soul. He met her gaze. Her smile fell and she traced his eyebrows.

"What's wrong?"

He shrugged and looked down. After the blow-up on the way to the fair a week or two ago, he didn't want to say anything. He couldn't shake this feeling in the pit of his stomach. "Wayne, tell me." She tipped his chin so he'd look at her.

"I-I just—" He released the back of her legs and leaned back against another hay bail. "I just don't like seeing you out there is all. I mean, you're lingering longer than you have before. Taking bigger risks. I'm just concerned. You said you did this for extra money. I helped out, and I can keep doing that. Whatever's needed."

"Wayne," she scolded him. "I'm grateful for your help, believe me it takes a huge amount of stress, but I don't need your money."

115

"I'm not trying to use my money to take anything away from you. I just want to help."

"You say that, but in the same breath you try to take clownin' away from me."

"I'm not takin' anything. I worry about you. Is that wrong?"

She pulled away and he got up to follow after her. She turned on him and poked him in the chest. "Like I don't worry about you. Like I like seeing you fall off a bull. Course not, but I'd never take it away from you. I'd never not be there for you."

He held up a hand, instantly regretting saying anything. "Desi—"

"No way, Wayne Frederick Dunbar." She knocked away his hand, which was on its way to cup her cheek.

"No need to get all official," he chuckled, going after her painted cheek again, this time with success. He moved some of the wild pink curly hair out of her face with a smile. He probably looked a damn fool arguing hot and heavy with someone dressed like she was. "I know I can't talk you out of it, so I won't even try." His voice was soft and low and it seemed to relax her a bit.

"Good," she cooed, grabbing his hands and putting them around her body. She kissed him on the nose and leaned into him. She took a deep breath before she spoke. "I'm really grateful for your help with my mom and you're right. Clowning was just a way for me to help out." She looked up into his eyes. "If you're helping then I don't need clowning."

His chest buoyed and relief washed over him. He kissed her on the forehead and pulled her into a strong hug.

"Thank you," she whispered.

He pulled away gazing into those cinnamon eyes. "You don't have to thank me for helping your mother."

She eyed him from under her lashes. "I'm not talking about that," she said. Mischief clung to the cadence of her voice.

He raised an eyebrow. "Then what?"

"Inviting me back to your home. I know that wasn't easy for you. I did some digging around and people don't seem to know where your little ranch is, which I'm sure is no mistake."

"You didn't tell 'em, did you?" The look on his face made her smirk.

"And share you? Never."

He laughed and allowed her to push him back to sit on the hay bale and straddle him. Her clown make-up was fuckin' with his head, but the silhouette of her body under his hands seemed to somehow counter the visual. "I'd like to thank you again," she whispered in his ear.

"For what?" He sounded like a drooling teenage boy, even to his own ears.

She pulled away and her creepy clown smile pulled at the corners as she rubbed down his chest, down his stomach, and over the growing bulge in his pants. "For what's to come."

Good Lord! And I thought I was bad. She's worse, and I love it. He rested back on the hay and let her undo his jeans, unzip them, part the flaps, reach in and retrieve his hardening penis. She slipped off his lap onto her knees and took him in her mouth. He let his head fall back, his mind falling far from his failure that day, far from their argument which he knew would never really end, far from anything but the sizzling energy that was wrapping his body with desire to be buried deep inside the woman's slick, wet lower lips.

| 25 | Bowels & Bad News |

"There is absolutely no talking during this test." Desi raised an eyebrow at Roy, receiving a mischievous smirk as he turned his eyes to his own paper. She frowned and looked back at the tutoring homework she was perusing in preparation for a session that evening.

She felt jittery inside, but she couldn't put her foot on it. She found her thoughts drifting to Wayne, drifting to their argument, if you would call it that. He had only responded honestly; she couldn't fault the man for that. It just made her upset. She was also just feeling on edge for some odd reason, like something was coming.

She smiled to herself thinking of something her grandma once said to her. The woman was superstitious. She had always had these strange feelings about all sorts of stuff. Most didn't pan out to be anything, but when it panned out, like the week her father had died, it was eerie. Made the hairs on the back of her neck stand on end, that kind of eerie.

Her attention moved to her phone when it buzzed, telling her she had a message. She opened it under her desk, as there was a no-phone policy in the school; especially during tests, for obvious reasons. She wanted to set a good example, but with everything going on the last few months with her mom, the principal made an exception for her.

It was from her boss who organized her clowning gigs. She felt the sting in her chest when she messaged him back to tell him she was not able to work the gig that coming week. She missed clowning, but she was making good money tutoring. It was more consistent now and of course safer. Wayne supported her tutoring, even brought her dinner when she stayed late to hold her sessions.

Her mind wandered when she thought about her time with Wayne at his childhood home. It was so peaceful so beautiful and warm. It seemed at ease there. When she saw him around the ranch she didn't realize how out of place he was in any other setting. She liked the way he looked at her, gazed at her like she was someone special.

"Miss Limb?"

She frowned, crashing back to reality, meeting Roy's brilliant blue eyes. "No talking during the test."

"But I'm raising my hand."

"While also talking." She exhaled, in no mood to deal with the child.

"Please, Miss Limb. It's important."

She exhaled. "What is it, Roy?"

"I need to go to the bathroom, like, really bad."

She frowned at him. "After you're done with your exam."

The boy farted loudly, eliciting an uproar of commotion, noise, and comments. "I can't wait. I'm gonna poop my pants."

She pushed up onto her feet, quieting the class. "Fine. Here, take the hall pass and go to the bathroom. No detours."

The boy got up from his desk, snatched the hall pass and sprinted out of the room.

"Okay, okay, show's over, back to your tests. No talking. Eyes on your own papers, please." Desi settled back behind her desk but only a moment later her phone distracted her again. She raised an eyebrow when she saw Wayne's number come up on her screen. She picked up the phone discreetly and made her way into the hallway.

"You better be dying, because if you're not, you will be when I see you again."

The man's deep laughter resonated through the phone. "I just wanted to hear your voice, honey."

She rolled her eyes, pushing down the buoyancy in her chest. "I'm hanging up right now." She was still shaking her head, the silly smile pulling up the corners of her lips when someone calling her name pulled her from that moment.

"Miss Limb?"

Desi looked over her shoulder to find Roy looking at her. Her eyebrows pulled together in concern when she saw the boy's green sweaty face.

"Good Lord Roy, you look terrible. You should go see the nurse."

The boy shook his head, one arm clutching his stomach. "I need to finish my spelling test."

She frowned, feeling bad for always being on the boy's case. "That doesn't matter right now." She poked her head into the classroom. "Turn in your tests face down on my desk and start on the math assignment. I have to take Roy to the nurse's office."

She wrapped her arms around the boy's shoulders as he clutched his middle and walked him down the hallway. She sat him in an open chair once they were in the office and explained the situation to the receptionist before perching on a chair next to him. "She's calling your mom."

He nodded. "Thanks."

"Of course."

Before she pushed up from her chair, the boy spoke up. "I actually studied for this spelling test. Certain I would have gotten a hundred."

The corner of her mouth lifted. "You'll have a chance to do a make-up."

He nodded. "Miss Limb?"

"Yes, Roy?" she said, looking at the sick boy with compassion.

"I know I don't always show it, but you're my favorite teacher."

She cocked her head to the side. That was the second time he said that. Didn't matter. It still made a smile spread across her face. "Careful what you say. In a day or two you'll be back in my class feeling well and wishing I wasn't working your brilliant brain so hard." She rested a hand on his shoulder. "Your mom will be here soon, okay?"

He smiled and nodded, then leaned his head back against the wall behind him as he closed his eyes.

When she returned to her classroom, she was pleasantly surprised to find her students silently working as if she'd never left at all.

She went back behind her desk and paused before sitting, when her phone started vibrating. She was getting another call.

She was going to string Wayne up by his toes if he—

She frowned when she saw it was her brother. "Derrick?" She pressed a finger to her ear and strolled to the door, closing it behind her. "Derrick, what is it?"

There was silence on the other end for a long moment until she heard sniffling. Heat rushed to her armpits and something clogged her throat. "Derrick, say something, Derrick!"

"It's ma. She's—" The man choked on the words as a deep sob wracked through him.

"W-what about her?" She was used to getting bad news about their mother, but she had seemed to be in good spirits, especially since Desi had visited with Wayne a few weeks ago.

"She—She's dead, Des. Ma's g-gone."

She gasped. The news hit her like a swift kick to the gut. She pressed her hand over her stomach and used the door as support as she slid to the ground. Her legs couldn't carry her; she couldn't stand. It was like her bones were turned to rubber, like her breath was stolen. She couldn't understand what he was saying, though what he said made perfect sense to her logically.

"Desi? Desi, are you okay? Des—" His voice broke off when she clicked the red button, ending the call. She didn't feel anything when she pushed the button or when she ignored him calling her back several times. She wasn't sure how long she sat there on the floor, just trying with her numb mind to grasp the conversation she just had.

After the phone was silent for a moment, it buzzed again. She looked down at the message from her clowning boss.

"Ya sure? Paying triple that night."

She inhaled, caring less about the money and more about the escape that clowning offered her. The sweat, the dirt, the high-octane energy-releasing stunts were real. This news, these lies that she had just heard weren't. When she was clowning, she wasn't a schoolteacher with a sick mom and a dead dad. She was just a silly clown doing a silly job. She could live outside herself. Most assumed she was a white man with nothing better to do than almost get bull's horns rammed up his ass. For some odd reason that sounded more appealing than whatever this so called reality was offering her.

She took a deep breath and started typing. "On second thought, I'll take the job."

| 26 | Reckless Abandon |

Wayne dismounted the angry bull and scurried to the pen's walls. Someone opened the door to let him out and closed it behind him. He looked for Desi before the rodeo started, figuring if she didn't have tutoring, she would be in those stands. Or at least that's what he assumed.

She hadn't been responding to his calls or messages. He thought the way they had left things in the barn a few days before was worth at least pickin' up her phone to respond to his message. She had answered the phone at school, sure, but then again she had sounded pretty peeved that he had called her at school in the first place.

He had every inclination to march right down to that school and get some answers after a couple days of her ignoring him, but he didn't want to get further in the hole. It was drivin' him bat shit crazy, though, it was.

The crowds' crescendo of frantic awe and a sea of rodeo clowns clambering toward the pen caught Wayne's attention. He turned and his heart fell to his feet when he saw his reckless little clown taunting the bull. The crowd was cheering, hootin' and hollerin'. The announcers in the booth were rattling on about her antics and Wayne's heart was thudding in his chest.

What was she even doing out there? She said she was done with it, done taking years off his life with worry over her getting killed.

What was she thinking? Is this her way of getting back at him for calling her at school?

She stopped running and faced the beast head-on, rotating her neck. Before he knew it, his face was plastered to the gate, looking on like everyone else. She was so far away, so vulnerable. Panic and helplessness filled him up from the middle of his gut to his throat. It stayed lodged there.

Anger floated through him. She was in danger, and there wasn't nothin' he could do. He pulled on the gate, but it was locked tight to keep the madness contained.

When the bull started charging, she stood up straight and blew air on her nails, sending the audience into fits of laughter. She dove out of the way just in time, stealing years off his life. He'd heard about stunts, but this? This was madness. He climbed up onto the gate and paused when the beast stopped and turned around to charge at her again. She was faced away from the bull, hyping up the crowd, who were cheering the loudest he'd heard since he and Rage last faced off.

He stopped climbing, straddling the top of the gate, when she did a tuck and dive out of the way moments before the big beast crashed past her. Other clowns were able to coax the animal to his exit on the opposite side of the pen. The audience seemed to exhale all at once, followed by uproarious cheers and chatter. The announcer in the booth was going wild with the events that had just unfolded, saying: "Ladies and gentlemen, the clown's gone wild. We weren't expecting a half-time show, but there you go!"

All the worry and fear inside his chest turned to anger, and all of it was focused on Desi, who was strolling toward the gate he was sitting on. Her attention was on the ground, and a serious look marred her painted features. He hopped off the gate right before they opened it up for her to exit. A bunch of other clowns crowded around her with shocked chatter and reenactments of some of her antics, but she paid them little mind.

"Desi," he called, following her to the barn.

She kept walking, either ignoring him on purpose, or just not hearing him. Either way, it didn't matter. Things needed to be talked about.

"Desi!" He grabbed her arm and turned her to face him.

She immediately yanked her arm from his hold.

"What the hell were you thinkin' out there?" He dug in, finally finding an outlet for the energy he had pinned up.

She frowned up at him, her dark eyes distant. "Who the hell do you think you're talkin' to?"

"You could have gotten yourself killed."

She rolled her eyes, turned and walked away. He caught up to her and grabbed her arm again. She snatched it away for a second time and turned on him like a bull in a pen.

"Don't touch me!" she shouted. Then her voice got low. "Don't ever touch me." She poked him in the chest with a gloved finger. "You can't domesticate me, *Wayne*." She said his name with such malice that he flinched. It reminded him of when they had first met. It had been enticing, but he thought they'd grown past that.

"What you talkin' 'bout? I never said nothin' about—"

" 'What the hell were you thinkin' in there?' " She mocked him. "I'm not your goddamn child or some subordinate little housewife that you can jerk around."

He was taken aback. Where was all this coming from? "Desi—"

"What is it really, huh?" She took a step toward him, her finger still poked into his chest, and he backed up. "Is it 'cause you're too old and fallin' apart? Maybe you feel your time comin' to an end, but you're too stubborn or dumb to just let go? Or is it that I'm a woman? Or is that I'm getting the attention you think is owed to you?"

He didn't do a good job tempering his anger. "I could care less about the attention and it sure as hell ain't got nothin' to do with you bein' a lady. It's that you're *my* lady just as I said before."

She retracted her sharp little finger and crossed her arms with a raised brow. "Well," she said, looking down at her boots. "You ain't gotta go worryin' about that anymore." She turned and hopped up on an oil drum on the side of the barn and looked down at him.

His chest clenched at the connotation. "Desi, I just want you safe—"

She climbed on top of the roof with little effort then turned back to look at him. "I don't need a master to keep me safe, to keep me from living." She walked away on the barn roof and disappeared over the peak.

125

A master? His insides burned with a mixture of feelings. He felt sick. *Master?* That was a heavy thing to say, considering who they were, where they were. *Is that really how she saw him?*

He rubbed his chest, as it suddenly seemed to sting a bit. He didn't understand her anger over something so small. He didn't understand why she had said the things that she said. Sure, he didn't like that she was a rodeo clown and he couldn't understand why she kept doing it, especially after she had agreed to stop. He had made sure to pay all her mother's doctor bills, so she couldn't need the money anymore. She didn't have to ask or hint or nothin', he had taken care of things free and clear. He didn't expect anything back. The only thing he had expected in return was for her to keep her word, for her to feel secure, for her to know that he had her back.

He rubbed his wrist, which was back to hurtin' again since she hadn't been takin' care of it like she had before they started their arguing'. He strolled into the barn and collapsed onto a bale of hay. *What did she mean I ain't gotta worry about that anymore? Did she just—*

He paused what he was doing and churned over the tumultuous series of events.

Did she just break up with me?

He refused to believe that. Surely him wantin' her to stop clownin' and him calling her while she was workin' couldn't be worth all that, unless he wasn't worth that to begin with. He cradled his face in his hands.

Is she really abandoning me? Leaving me? He'd done some fucked up things in his life, 'specially to the fairer sex, but he knew what he'd done when they came after him.

He'd been a little overbearing with his desire to keep her out of the pen, but she was steamin' hot. It seemed overkill. Maybe he just needed to let her simmer. Problem was, he wasn't good at waitin'. Wasn't good at all, but if that's what needed doin' to get her back in his arms, he'd do it.

| 27 | Wilted Flower |

Wayne knocked the woman's hand away as she approached him, yet again, with a fine-toothed comb.

"I'm a cowboy, not some God-damn Elvis impersonator." He frowned in the mirror at the gelled-down hair.

"Mr. Dunbar—"

"Don't Mr. Dunbar me. Just go, please." It was day three of shooting the commercials and he was sick of it all. To top it all off, he still couldn't get Desi on the phone. After her blow-up at the rodeo a few days before, it had been radio silence. He didn't like the way they had left things. It didn't feel right, or maybe he was just deluded into thinking she would want anything to do with him once she calmed down.

There was a knock on the doorframe to his dressing room. He had a God damn dressing room. What the hell had life come to? He was a cowboy, not some Hollywood actor. That's where he was though: *Hollywood.*

He cringed.

He needed his Texas and even more, he needed his woman to stop ignoring him.

"Kyle." He was relieved to see the man and not some director or producer, and certainly not hair and fuckin' makeup. "Did you get Desi on the phone?"

Kyle pushed his glasses up on his face and walked cautiously into the room. "No, bu—"

"Wayne, Wayne, Wayne, Wayne." In swanned Liz, her blonde hair perfectly styled to fit her small head. She breezed past Kyle as if he wasn't even there and took a perch on a stool next to Wayne.

"I know you're restless, but we're almost done. This is the last day and then you can get back to the countryside." She frowned at him, reached over to the vanity behind her, got a comb and scraped the wild strands into place. "Things might seem like they don't feel authentic, but that's because we're in Hollywood. Wait until you see the finished commercial. It'll be just perfect."

She put a hand over his and he looked down at it then back up at her. A familiar warmth stirred in his insides, reminding him how long it'd been since he was intimate with his girl. Might have been wrong, the thought that crossed his mind, but turning Liz over had nothin' to do with what he felt in his chest, only what he felt in his pants. He needed to release the tension of every damn thing. "I just need you to hold in there a little longer. Can you do that?" She rubbed her hand from his knee up his thigh but stopped when Kyle cleared his throat.

"I'll need a moment alone with my client, please. He'll be ready in ten."

The woman bit her bottom lip and held Wayne's eyes before getting up and swaying out of the room. That was another damn problem. Liz had always been flirtatious from the beginning, but the past couple of days it seemed like she was even more so. More touches, on the shoulder, the arm, just now his leg and his inner thigh. She had to know what it did to a man. With everything going on with Desi, the woman was fuckin' with his head.

Desi's mother's words floated through his mind, which always sobered him up. He chose Desi and he wouldn't let anything jeopardize that, not even her silence. But she had said she was done with him in as many words. It made his chest burn just thinking about it. He was refusing to accept it, but what if she'd already moved on?

Kyle sat down where the woman had been. "What I was saying was, there's a good reason why Desi might be distant." He held his phone out to face Wayne, who read the page that was up on the screen. He took the phone in awe. He couldn't believe it. He frowned up at Kyle, his chest filled with anger and hurt.

"Why didn't she tell me?"

He shrugged, taking his phone back from Wayne. "We all deal with grief in our own way."

Wayne stood. "I need to get to her, whether she wants me there or not."

Kyle stood and placed a hand on his shoulder. "You will. Once we finish here for the day, we're on the first plane out. I'll work on getting our flights switched around."

"Thanks." Wayne frowned. "Say, Kyle, we've known each other since elementary and you've been with me since I started, even though we weren't good friends back in school. Why?"

Kyle smirked and pushed his glasses up on his face. "I see talent, work ethic, passion." He clapped Wayne on the shoulder hard, and it made him wince but smile. "I might dream about riding a bull, but I don't have the gall to do it. Navigating fame? No thank you, but this, what I do? I'm good at it. Plus it pays really, really well."

*

Desi smashed the dirt with the trowel. She wiped the tears that streamed down her cheek away with her shoulder and kept digging. She should have been in school, but the principal had sent her home for bereavement after she had an encounter with one of the other teachers. And by one of the other teachers, she meant Jen. The wench had the nerve, in the same breath as she wished her condolences for her loss, had been asking after Wayne for some damn gossip she'd heard about them been broken up.

Her heart ached at the compounded loss. The things she had said to him—

She choked back regret, choked back sadness, choked back pain. Her mother always said some things said couldn't be unsaid, couldn't be forgiven. She hadn't even meant them like they came out, but it was too late.

She held onto her anger because that was the only emotion she was willing to let in at the moment. He had smothered her, tried to make her quit clownin'. That type of relationship wasn't what she wanted. She really wanted freedom. What was stopping her now? What was standing in her way?

Nothing.

Wayne was the only obstacle and he was gone.

Her chest gripped her breath at that thought. He was gone. Gone. Just like her mother, just like her father. Taken from her, stolen from her too soon.

She winced and wiped more tears away. Truth was, she was trying to mend her own wound. The one that she was responsible for. The hurt look on his face was a still frame in her mind.

In her current moment, she just felt horrible. She held her stomach and dry heaved. How could she want him to hurt like she did? What kind of wretch was she? She had handled things all wrong with him. He deserved better far better than a wilted flower. She knew that eventually she would have to face him, face her own actions, but she dreaded it. What if he dismissed her? What if he had already found someone to warm his bedsheets? It was no more than she deserved for her behavior.

"Oh, mama." She cradled her face in her dirty hands and let the tears that she held in for so long leak out. First her father, now her mother. God had taken them, claimed his children, but Wayne? Her sobs deepened, flooding her heart with her emotions. That loss was all on her.—

"Desi?"

She looked up when the heavy, low vibrations of Wayne's familiar voice caressed her ears. Her vision was blurred by the tears, and before she could wipe them away his strong arms were around her.

She clung to him with all she had. The smell of tobacco, mint, and sandalwood encircled her, presenting a sense of familiarity that went far beyond the short time she'd known the man. The liquid still streamed out of her eyes and seeped into his thick sweater. Her body shook with her sobs and yet he still held her. He was saying things she couldn't hear, but the soft rumble of his voice was a comfort that she was missing. He kissed her hair a few times, just letting her release it all.

She hadn't really cried since her father was snatched from her and she had a lot to purge. Over fifteen years of pent-up tears had left her, several moments later, exhausted.

Wayne picked her up, and she let him. She held fast around his neck. He carried her into the house, up the stairs and set her on a chair in her room. He removed her dirty clothes down to her underwear and bra, took her to the bed, put her under the covers, took his clothes off down to his underwear, got in next to her and cradled her body snugly against his.

"Wayne? I—"

"Shhh," he interrupted. "We can talk later. Now, you need to get some rest."

| 28 | Removing Thorns |

"I thought you'd left."

Wayne looked up from the newspaper and sipped his coffee. "You're not getting off that easy."

She rubbed her forehead and looked down at her bare feet. She slept all day the day before, from when he found her weeping in her garden until it was almost three in the afternoon that next day.

He frowned, his attention on her attire when she strolled into the rather comfortable porch. She was wearing the sweater he'd left on the chair upstairs. She always kept her house warm to his liking, but he liked the way she looked in his clothes.

He tried to clear the possessive thoughts about her being his and all, seeing as how their last conversation had gone.

She sat next to him on the couch with her feet tucked under her. "Wayne," she said, facing him. "I'm sorry."

"Desi—"

"No, no." She exhaled. "I need to say this." Her eyes, already puffy from all the crying the previous day, started welling up again, the tears spilling over. "I'm sorry for what I said to you. I-I didn't even mean it. I was just angry about ma, but that doesn't matter. There's no excuse for my behavior."

There was a long silence that filled the space between them. Wayne's attention was on his fumbling fingers. "Why'n't you tell me 'bout your mama?" He looked up at her from under his lashes. "I understand your pain. I lost my parents too. They were too young. I was too young. Joey Lou prolly doesn't even remember Ma."

She shrugged, her eyes finding her lap. "I-I don't know. It just didn't feel real."

He let the silence hang in the air between them, waiting for her to continue. Eventually she did.

"Even when I saw her body later on a video chat with Derrick, it didn't seem real. I was just talking to her the other day. I heard her voice just a week ago. I heard her laugh, she scolded me for something, we saw one of your jean commercials on the television and she was making a comment. I just didn't understand what had happened. I couldn't stop myself from wondering if I did all I could to keep her here. If she was happy, if she was comfortable—"

She broke off into sobs. He couldn't sit there and watch her in pain, so he pulled her into him and she rested, curled up in a ball, at his side. He rubbed her arms, hurting for her loss. Suddenly the whirlwind of questions and accusations he had for her were of little importance. His bruised ego and aching heart belonged only to her. If he could take her pain, he would without thinking twice on it.

Her mother's words floated through him and he felt them down to his very core:

'I knew without a shadow of a doubt if he had only one breath left in his body, he'd give it to me if only to see me smile one last time.'

"You did everything you could do, and she knew that."

She pulled away to look into his eyes. Her flushed face, damp cheeks and red eyes made his chest constrict. He cupped her cheek in his palm and she nuzzled into it. "I don't know what you said to my mom, but she told me you were a good man. That sort of praise doesn't come easily from Eileen Limb." She frowned and looked down for a moment in thought. He kissed her forehead and squeezed her closer. He liked her ass resting in his palm, that familiar floral fragrance, and her weight on his lap was an ill-timed distraction.

"Your mama is a good woman."

They set there in silence for a long while his thoughts, somewhere in there floating to their last interaction. "Desi, why'd you say what you did at the rodeo?"

She let out a long exhale and pulled away from him to wrap her arms around herself. "I-I sabotage everything because I— because I was hurting. I knew I was wrong, but I didn't want to stop. Running seemed the only way to avoid losing you too. Then I realized I didn't want to lose you. I'm—" She broke off, swallowing before she looked back into his eyes. "Can you forgive me?"

He took in a long breath and let it go just as slow. "What you said really hurt."

Her bottom lip quivered as she looked up at him from under her lashes. "I know I—" He silenced her with a finger pressed to her lips.

"What I really want to know is, is that how you see me? Am I some oppressive overlord, some *master*?" He swallowed the thick word down his tightening throat. "That's keeping you enslaved? Trapped? Keeping you from living your life?"

She looked down shame and regret washed her features. "No." She looked up at him briefly. "I truly don't. I said those things because I—" She paused. "Because I knew they would hurt you."

There was physical pain in him, hearing her say that. "Why would you want to do that?"

"Because I was hurting and I wanted someone else to feel my pain. It was wrong, so, so wrong, inexcusably wrong. I know that."

"Inexcusable, yes." He held his voice steady because he felt the depth of her sincerity and all he wanted to do was tell her that everything was okay. But he also never wanted that toxic bullshit to ever happen again. "But not unforgivable if you promise me one thing." He paused until she looked up to meet his eyes again. He swallowed to temper the zing through his chest at her vulnerability, at her hope.

"What's that?"

"You can't ever say nothin' like that to me again, ever. I'd never say anything like that to you, Desi, cause it'd never even cross my mind." That was the truth.

She nodded. "Okay, I promise. Never again."

"Desi?"

"Hmm?" She finally met his eyes again.

"Kiss me."

She sat up in his lap and took his face in her palms, holding his eyes. Her gaze fell to his mouth and lingered there for an extended

134

period of time before she slowly descended to touch their lips together. Soft and gentle at first, then she slid her fingers to the back of his head, pulling them through his hair. She angled her face over his and leaned into the kiss, seeming to pour her life into him.

She moaned, a sensual feminine sound that sent blood coursing straight to his pants. He pulled away from her, grabbing her hands that had somehow started undoing the buttons on his shirt.

"Wayne," she whined, the sound so arousing it took everything in him to stay focused. He was very aware of the length of time since he had last had her perfection wrapped around him. But this wasn't about him, not at its core. It was about her mourning. He cupped her face and pressed their foreheads together.

"Sex isn't going to heal your pain or help you mourn your loss, honey."

Her moist eyes met his after she swallowed. "I just want to be close to you."

He placed her palm on his chest and pulled her head to lay on him before he kissed her hair and nuzzled his face in her mass of tight curls. "I'm here, darlin' and I'm not goin' nowhere."

| 29 | Faced With Loss |

Desi pulled the short black veil over her face and took in a deep breath as she gazed at herself in the mirror. She felt it. The black, the loss, the unknown.

She had always had her mother. She couldn't imagine what life would be like without her. She couldn't believe that if she had children one day, they would never know their grandmother.

It was so heavy. it was still difficult to grasp. Even though she knew the truth, it still felt like it was happening to someone else.

She descended the stairs. Every movement seemed deliberate, laborious.

Wayne stood up from the couch and turned to face her. The corner of her mouth lifted when she took him in, wearing an all-black suit with a matching black tie. Her eyebrows raised. She'd never seen him dressed up like that before. As usual, he was handsome.

"How you feelin'?" he wanted to know, pulling her into a loose embrace when she finally made it to the first floor.

"I'm here."

He nodded and kissed her hair. "Are you ready to go?"

She nodded. "Should or we'll be late."

They drove all the way to Houston in silence. Her mind was everywhere in the past and present, everywhere except for the future.

Mostly because she didn't know what it would hold with her mother gone.

It was one of those weird things. She knew one day her mom would be gone like so many before, but it had always seemed so far away. She should have given the woman another hug or another kiss or told her how much her daughter loved her one more time.

Desi looked down at Wayne's hand in her lap, palm up, waiting for her. She looked over at the man and let her head fall to the side in thought. He kept glancing from the road to her. There was remorse in his eyes, concern, care.

What the hell had she done to deserve this man? He was so good to her, even when she wasn't so good to him. She looked back down at his hand and let her fingertips trace some of the lines in his palm. She outlined the shape of his thumb and glided her finger from his wrist to the tips of his fingers before she settled her hand in his.

He let his fingers close over her hand but said nothing. Nothing to comfort her, or to assure her that everything would be okay.

Good.

She was tired of hearing that. Tired of other people putting off their awkward energy to her. No one really knew what to say at times like these because, well, they weren't sure how the other person would take it. Didn't know what to say, but still saw fit to open their mouths. All she wanted was silence, and somehow he seemed to know that.

The entire thing was surreal, honestly. Viewing the body that looked like her mother, or kind of. The corpse was smaller, more fragile than her mom was. It was strange seeing her in makeup, since the woman rarely wore it. She watched them lower the casket into the ground.

Before the body was all the way into the hole, her vision blurred over with tears. A deep sorrow washed over her so strongly that her legs gave way.

Strong familiar arms accompanied by a familiar scent grabbed her before she hit the ground, holding her upright. She curled into his strong body and let the sobs roll through her. The sobs came with varying emotions, fear, anger and sadness. They were switching back and forth, up and down, consuming her mind. Consuming her will.

Gone.

Her mother was gone. She felt the truth more than she'd felt it at any other time in the past several days.

She'd never see her mother smile again, or hear her laugh. Be locked in her intense gaze or hear her strong opinions. She'd never lose to her in cards again, or hear her tell her how proud she was of her daughter. She'd never have to change another diaper, or pay another bill, get her any more water or fluff another pillow for the woman.

Gone.

She wasn't sure why there was a gathering after the funeral was over. Everyone was miserable, and those who weren't, she wanted to punch in the throat. She sipped her water instead. She could feel it under her skin, the need to escape. That wasn't good; she knew that. Running away just made things worse.

She recalled her father. She had been a child when he died, and she hadn't really faced that pain until she'd talked about it with Wayne in the car. She couldn't let that much time pass before she faced this sorrow too.

Wayne walked back in the parlor and kneeled next to her chair. "Sorry about the interruption again."

"If you need to handle something, please go ahead."

He grabbed her hand and took a deep breath. "It can wait."

She shook her head. "Go on, please. I think I want to be alone anyway."

He frowned gazing at her steadily. "Are you sure, Desi? I don't mind makin' them wait."

The corner of her mouth lifted and she cupped his cheek tenderly. "I know you don't. I insist. I think I need a day or two to figure somethings out. I'll see you in L.A. at the end of the week."

He looked down. "You don't have to go——"

"Shh." She placed her fingertips over his lips. "I want to. Besides," she said, mustering up a little joyous energy. "I refuse to miss you dressed in a three-piece suit." She leaned down and kissed his smiling face. "Now go."

He nodded, stood, kissed her on the forehead and left the room.

Gone.

He was gone, but it wasn't so final this time. She'd see him again in a few days. She'd see him again, but before then there were so many things she needed to do.

| 30 | Civilized Humans |

Wayne paced back and forth in front of the museum where the damned red-carpet gala thing was happening. He had wanted to travel with Desi, but she needed to stay in Houston for the reading of her mother's will, which he had offered to attend with her despite his other commitments. Everything as of late had been focused on the upcoming match of his career: Wayne Versus Rage.

He laughed at all the hype it was setting up to get. He'd been in the pen with the bull several times before like a bunch of other riders yet somehow people liked associating the two of them together.

His thoughts shifted back to Desi.

He hated seeing her struggle through the technical stuff, but her brother seemed to be a big help. He checked his watch. He was early. Nerves did that to him. He wasn't sure why he was so nervous. He pulled at the bowtie, near choking himself in the process. He looked around at the skyscrapers that filled L.A.'s downtown like foreign trees, glass aliens meant to smush him under their metal feet.

He didn't do too well in the city, and fancy to-dos just weren't his calling, but he had given his word that he would do it by signing the damn contract, so by gum he was gonna do it.

His mental rant stopped when the limo he had hired to pick her up from their hotel pulled up. The chauffeur reached her door before he could get to it, but no one was there to catch his jaw before it hit the ground.

She stepped out of the limo, one golden heel first, and then a fire-hydrant red, flowy dress caught the breeze before he actually saw her face emerge from the interior.

She looked flawless, her curls pulled up in an immaculate crown on her head. A piece of jewelry rested on her forehead and the chain was wrapped around her hair. Her makeup was subtle but left her with a golden glow that stole his nerves, his breath, and his heart too.

He offered his arm and she took it with a big smile, pulling up her cheeks as she eyed him up and down.

"Don't you look like a civilized human being."

He leaned into her. "Don't let the penguin suit fool you, darlin'. The rodeo ain't never gonna leave me."

She smiled up at him as they walked up the stairs. "I should hope not."

*

Desi enjoyed the finery. People she'd never thought she'd even be in the same room with were interested in knowing who she was. Interviews, which were for Wayne, seemed to keep pulling them apart. He was charming and short with his answers, but everyone seemed to love him, which they should. His commercials were playing on large screens around the place, and boy, did he look like a supermodel. Gruff and untamed, dangerous, a rogue, *her* rogue cowboy. She was proud of his accomplishments, for seeing him getting his due.

She'd never seen him in a suit before, and boy, did he look handsome. He could easily be some billionaire CEO mingling with the common folk. She smiled at the thought.

After a fancy dinner with more courses than she cared to count, followed by some dancing, she'd made her way out on the veranda overlooking a spectacular garden. Wayne had gone to get punch and had probably gotten caught up with people vying for his attention.

His scent wrapped around her, along with his arm, when he suddenly hugged her from behind. He handed her the punch with the other hand before kissing her on the neck.

"Thanks for agreeing to come to this with me. I know there's a lot else goin' on."

She smiled at him over her shoulder, catching his grey eyes in the artificial lighting. "It meant a lot to you." She set the punch down on the thick concrete railing and turned to face him.

He kissed her on the forehead. "You mean a lot to me."

She felt it. She felt his words down to her bones, deep in her chest, surrounding her soul. "How did everything go in Houston?"

She shrugged. She'd hoped she wouldn't have to think about that. "Went fine."

His brows pulled together. "What happened?"

She shrugged away from him, which was more difficult than she had anticipated. "It's not a big deal."

"That means it is a big deal." His warm hand rested on her lower back and he walked up beside her. "You can tell me when you're ready."

She glanced at him and exhaled. "Just my brother and uncle fighting over some of mom's stuff."

He frowned. "Was there anything you wanted that you didn't get?"

"No. It's not even about all that. I ended up having to settle some silly nonsense. I mean, my mom just died and they're fighting over some material bullshit." She pressed her palm to her forehead. He rubbed up her back and pulled her into him. She leaned on him. "It's just, all this got me thinkin'."

He stopped rubbing her arm for a minute before asking, "About what?"

She exhaled. "I-I could have done a lot of different things for extra money instead of clowning: tutoring, private lessons, after-school programs, but I chose clowning because I used to do gymnastics." The corner of her mouth lifted and she drifted off to some place in the past. "My dad would always take me to lessons, and he helped me practice. When he passed, my mom couldn't afford to keep it up, so I had to stop. I guess I missed the freedom, the fun of the challenge." She looked at him as he gazed down at her.

"I didn't know you were in gymnastics. Guess it makes sense why you're so agile and athletic."

She smiled. "Yeah, I know. There are so many things that remind me of Papa, but not saying those things won't make him come back so I might as well say them."

He nodded. "It's okay to miss them. I miss my folks all the damn time."

"Am I interrupting something?" Their attention went to a slender blonde woman with a pixie cut who sauntered out onto the concrete walk.

"I'm not sure I introduced you two yet. Liz, this is my lady, Desiree Limb. Desi, this is Elizabeth Burns, the brains behind this whole operation." Desi shook the woman's hand, noticing her firm grip. She'd seen the fairy-like woman making her way around the place with an eye-crinkling smile on the entire evening. It was hard not to see her. She had a magnetic presence. Power rolled off her in waves.

"Nice to meet you." Desi presented a wide smile.

"The pleasure is mine. Uh, how long have you two been together?" The woman's attention was on Wayne.

"Uh, some months."

"Hmm." The woman nodded and presented a forced smile that almost looked like the real thing. "Well, I hope you're enjoying the festivities. When you have a minute, we have a couple of photo requests from some investors."

"Sure. I'll be there in a few minutes."

"Excellent." She discreetly looked Desi over and raised a fine eyebrow before turning and walking away.

"What the hell was that?" Desi asked after the woman disappeared inside.

"What was what?"

"What exactly is she the brains behind?" Desi crossed her arms over her chest.

"S-she was the lead from the marketing firm. She orchestrated everything."

Mhm, I bet, Desi thought. She might not be an expert on men, fancy galas or million-dollar marketing campaigns, but she knew women. "Why was she asking when we started dating?" She raised her chin and focused on him, the possibilities racing through her mind. They had been broken up for a small time there. *Had he found another woman? Why would I be upset about it if he had?* She had no right to be. She had made her bed, and this was a part of sleeping in it.

"We didn't do nothin', if that's what you're implying. I'm not going to lie and say it didn't cross my mind when the two of us were fightin', though. When you left me in limbo, not knowin' if you'd ever be back."

She swallowed, upset at the tears welling up behind her eyes. She wasn't sure why. She turned away from him and walked back toward the concrete railing.

"Desi, I didn't say that to hurt you."

She moved so he couldn't clasp her waist. "I'm not mad at you."

"Well that's not altogether true, now is it?"

"But it is true." She wrapped her arms around herself as the breeze picked up. "It just reminds me of that entire series of events and I'm ashamed at how it all went down."

"We talked through that already." He was close, but he didn't make a move to touch her. When she looked over her shoulder at him his hands were tucked in his pockets. "I forgave you. We moved on."

"Yeah, but I don't think I forgave myself yet."

"But you have to, Desi."

She faced forward and wiped the tears away. "I know I will. Hey, why don't you go take your pictures. Don't want to keep your rabid fans waiting." She smiled over her shoulder at him.

He took a few steps closer, kissed her on the head and wrapped his jacket over her shoulders. Before he went inside he said, "I'm a simple man. All I want is to move on forward with my beautiful woman. That's all."

| 31 | Complete Trust |

"She likes you."

Wayne blinked, trying to focus on the road in the congested city. Did he ever mention that he hated cities? They showed humanity at its worst, removed from nature, from fresh air, from peace and quiet. "Huh?" He brought his attention to his lady sitting in the rented truck next to him.

"The blonde woman with the great calves."

He glanced over at her quickly. "Blonde woman?" He was honestly lost. He'd been overwhelmed with all the people wanting him to go here, go there, photos, handshakes, introductions, all things he knew were good for his career, but the whole time he just wanted his woman, a horse, and a nice trail to wander down. Things had been feelin' real disjointed lately between them and he didn't like it one bit.

"Elizabeth Burns, the brains behind the whole operation?" She mocked his introduction of his account manager from earlier that evening.

He smirked over at her, noticing the irritation in her voice when she said the other woman's name. He liked when she claimed him even if through jealousy. It felt good knowing that she was there and paying attention. "Told you, nothin' going on there," he said, recalling confessing that he'd thought about it. It was more about convenience than actually finding the woman as his heart's temptation. Her willingness in his time of weakness, pain, and confusion was what had been attractive to him then.

"She likes you." He caught her side-eyeing him with a look of mischief on her face.

His insides did that slow-moving swim at the sensual quality of her voice. "Hate to break it to you, sweetheart, but lots of women want a piece of your man." He reached over and offered his hand to her with his palm up on the middle armrest.

She looked down at it for a moment, seeming to be sizing it up, then she slid her slender appendage right where it fit perfectly in his. He felt his insides stir at the feel of her skin on his, but oddly enough, he also felt himself relax.

"I don't much like her." She confessed.

He laughed and glanced over at her briefly. "Well, I don't much like you clownin' but do you hear me complainin'?"

"Ha!" She said looking out her window. "Subtle."

He laughed a little letting her slender fingers roll through his larger ones. There was a bout of silence that he let sit there.

"Suppose now with ma gone, I don't need clowning, huh?"

He laughed a little before he glanced over as his beautiful companion.

"What you laughin' for?"

Damn she was pretty with her brow furrowed scoldin' him. "Think both of us know you can't stay out of that dirt stage no more than I can stay off a bull."

"Ha! There is no comparison. I can do it and I will. Can promise you that. Eileen Limb was my reason and now she's gone."

He felt her energy shift with her voice on the last part; so, he looked over at her again. He didn't have a lot of time to decipher her expression. He saw sadness, which he expected. She just lost someone so dear to her. It was fresh on her heart. He remembered when he lost his mama too. Sometimes it still sent a twinge of pain through his chest.

He exhaled and squeezed her dainty hand still kept in his. "Well, you not clownin' sure would ease my worry. I'll tell you that."

"Would it?"

He raised an eyebrow at the play in her voice and glanced over at her quickly to find the mischief he thought he heard.

"Mhm, that's right." She reached over with her free hand and traced it from his knee up to his inner thigh. A buoyant energy floated in his chest. He tried to steady his breathing, but suddenly the hotel was too far away and all the damn humans, lights, and turns standing between him and a room alone with his lady were bound to get knocked off the map. "Don't go causin' a car accident now."

She giggled facing forward again after retracting her arm. She leaned over, rested her head on his shoulder, and let out a long exhale.

His heart swelled. Such a simple motion, so meaningful. Complete trust, completely resting in him, in his strength. From Desi, it felt like a silent surrender. What was she surrendering exactly? He didn't quite know, but he had a few thoughts on what he hoped it was.

He kissed the back of her hand, enjoying the tangle of her fingers soft and small in his palm as he stroked them. She used her free hand to stroke up and down his arm.

"I missed you," she whispered into the silent car.

He turned his head slightly to press a kiss into her abundant coils. "I missed you too, baby."

No more words needed to be spoken for a calm ease to settle in the remaining space. He could feel her heat, hear her soft breathing, hear his own. Her soft floral scent found home in his brain and the whirlwind of feelings from the event was replaced with a soft yearning for home. Home was more than just his ranch back in Texas. It was also the woman right next to him.

Several minutes later, he tossed the car keys to the valet, took his woman's hand, and led her inside the hotel lobby. His chest lifted when he noticed the passersby admiring them. He knew she was nothing less than stunning, and she was all his.

They rode up the elevator in silence, each watching the numbers. The metal shaft pulled them up to the penthouse suite, kindly provided by his new partners at the marketing company.

"This view never gets old." A sweet smile pulled up the corner of her mouth as she let go of his hand and walked into the space. She wandered over to the large floor to ceiling windows.

"Look at all the lights," she said, her voice filled with wonder.

147

He told himself he was going to just sit back and watch her, but somehow his feet ended up carrying him to stand behind her. He clasped her shoulders and she leaned back against him. Her soft, pliable body against him after being so far gone for such a period of time made him want her naked in his arms.

He leaned down and kissed her shoulder. She looked back at him over her shoulder, her parted lips a sweet temptation. Her gaze fell to his mouth and he looked at her too. Her lush full lips were still painted with lipstick, a red seduction. He stroked her jaw with his thumb and clasped the nape of her neck, gazing into her eyes before settling on her mouth.

He leaned down and pressed his lips against hers, eliciting a sigh. She turned to face him and linked her slender arms around his neck. She was in his hold now. His hands ran up and down her cocktail dress until his fingertips found the zipper, which he eased down. She pulled away for a moment to let the dress fall over her sweet, soft curves and pool at her feet on the floor.

"God damn," he said before he could process that he'd even said anything. His eyes were devouring her full breasts, the tops of which were the only thing visible under the lace bra. Her flat stomach and smooth chocolate skin seemed to glow under the interior lights.

He slid one hand around her and unhooked the bra. He pulled it away from her with both hands and pushed the panties over her hips, falling to a kneeling position before her perfect nudity.

He pressed a kiss to her stomach then dragged his tongue from her belly button down to her pretty bare lower lips. He lifted her leg and she leaned against the metal window mullion behind her. She grabbed his shoulder for stability when he placed one of her legs on his shoulder so he could gain access to the prize.

He swallowed, her unique scent hitting him.

He kissed her pussy and she groaned, rolling her head back against the glass.

Perfect.

All the insanity that had ensued over the past several weeks made this moment mean so much more to him. He hadn't had his woman since her mother had passed away and so much had happened since then. Hurtful things had been said, talked through, and on his part forgiven.

All he wanted was her.

He closed his mouth over her sex and suckled her as if this was the last time he would ever get to taste her, have her, feel her, hear her sighs and sensual moans.

He deepened the licks from the crux of her sex up to her clit and swirled around it before he suckled the outer lips. He moaned against her when her fingers combed into his short hair. His name passed her lips in a sensual, seductive sigh that made his own throbbing need press harder against the confining dress pants.

He pulled away from her sex, picked her up in his arms and carried her into the bedroom where he laid her on the bed. He grabbed a condom from his back pants pockets, shed all the clothes as quickly as he could and climbed into the bed, settling between her legs where it felt like he belonged. She wrapped one thigh over his hips and stroked the sides of his face. The hair had started to grow back there, so it felt good when she lightly scraped her fingers along his jaw.

He covered his penis with the condom before he slipped between her slippery, juicy lower lips his mouth had suckled only moments before.

He inhaled the splendid feeling of being submerged in her moisture. The sensation filled his brains with endorphins. He just wanted to settle there, wrapped up in his flower's scent, her warmth, the soft pliable, firm feel of her body under his own.

He kissed her full lips once, deepening the kiss when she pulled him down toward her. He pulled out then eased back in feeling a thrill when she gasped in his mouth. Her moans and whispered affirmations encouraged him to increase his pace, to revel in the feel of her vagina as it produced even more liquid to aid in their pleasure. It was almost too much; it was so slippery, even with the condom.

He ground his teeth, wanting to feel her find an end before he did, but he wasn't sure it was possible to hold off. It had been so long since he'd had her.

She clasped her arms around his middle, clutching on to him as he slammed in and out of her, wild and frantic.—

"Aww fuck," he said before the overpowering rush of completion propelled him from that plane of existence into another.

| 32 | That Beautiful View |

She stuffed the papers into her soft leather briefcase and placed the pens and pencils she'd been using for grading back in the cup at the corner of her desk. She strolled to the door and turned to glance back at her classroom before clicking off the lights.

She shut the door, her mind wandering to the one and only irritating person in her life who she also cared about more than anyone. Through her tantrums and resistance, overwhelming fear, sadness, and moments of peace and joy; there Wayne stood. His persistence and love was what she needed through such a touch time. Watching in terror as her mother deteriorated was the hardest thing she ever did. Until recently she couldn't acknowledge that.

"Have a good weekend, Desi."

"You too Aubrey." Desi waved at her friend as she left out the front door of the school and started walking home, enjoying the warm spring afternoon. The school year would be coming to an end soon and she'd be able to enjoy a hot but work-free few months. A bittersweet feeling wrapped around her body.

With her mother g—

Her mind choked over the thought.

With her mother gone. She took a deep breath on that. She didn't need to work herself to the bone. Her loving and obnoxious boyfriend—

She paused over the thought. It was strange how things had progressed with Wayne so quickly. *Boyfriend, partner*. That's what he was to her. Still strange sometimes.

She shook that thought and moved back to the one that had conjured it up. Her loving and obnoxious partner paid for all sorts of things that she didn't ask him to, like her mortgage, her energy bill. No more car notes, no more student loans. He didn't bat an eyelash, and she didn't have to ask. Often times she wouldn't even know he did it until it was long gone and done.

Obnoxious? Mhm.

She scolded him for it at first, but he made it very clear that caring for her was what he enjoyed doing; so, she swallowed all her upbringing and independent woman rhetoric and let the man do it.

She was surprised at how good it felt. How good it felt to not have to worry, to be able to do things with her earnings that she wanted without feeling guilty that she wasn't helping out enough. She was grateful but perhaps didn't show it as readily as she could have to Wayne.

When she got home, she suddenly didn't want to be there. Every time she looked around she saw something else she needed to do: dishes, laundry, fix the squeaky doors upstairs and make sure the porch screens were ready for mosquitoes. She loved her home, but she was feeling restless. Besides, it was too fine a day to waste it on menial tasks.

Wayne warned her in L.A. that he was going to be busy preparing for his bout with Rage. Currently, he was in Dallas on some kind of campaign or interview circuit or something, as it seemed the entire state was getting all hyped up about their match.

Before he left, he made sure to set a time to see her on Sunday where she would finally get to cook him dinner, payment for her losing the race on their second date. That entire thing felt like an eternity ago, maybe because so much had happened in such a short time since.

She tossed her school stuff near her desk nook and changed into riding clothes. Yes, riding sounded like a pleasant thing to do. The weather certainly was screaming it with the warm breeze and setting sun.

She headed out to the Chapmans' to take Beauty out for a ride up to the canyon.

"Desiree! It's been a little while since I've seen you up here. Heard about your time in Los Angeles. How are you farin'?"

The corner of her lips pulled up as she strolled into the barn. "I'm good, Ray. Think I just need a short ride with Beauty if she's up for it."

The handsome older man smiled. "Funny you ask, I was just about to take the old girl out for a little exercise."

Desi strolled right up to the lovely mare and stroked down her face. The horse nuzzled her face against Desi's nibling a bit on her nose making her giggle. "There girl. I missed you too. You want to take a little ride?" The horse moved her hooves as if she were replying.

The man set the brush down from grooming one of the other horses and grabbed a saddle off a nearby hook. "How's Wayne doing? Seem like I can't look anywhere without seein' him on the television."

She smiled, more to herself. "Funny you mention that, because he's in Dallas now doing something in preparation for the big rodeo."

The man nodded. "Ah, yes, everyone's talking about it." He placed the saddle on Beauty's back and Desi helped him strap it down. Either of them could have easily saddled the horse, but sometimes teamwork was nice. "The battle of the season, Rage versus Wayne." The man laughed. They're selling bobbleheads for it. I know it's a waste of money, but I bought one anyway."

She giggled. She found it hard to believe that the practical man would spend money on such a trinket. "I'm sure that bobblehead is more accurate than the collectors' dolls of him."

He let out a robust laugh as she reenacted the wiggly-neck motion of a bobblehead.

"Yep. That's right!" He laughed some more before finishing up with the saddle. "There we go. I think the old girl is ready whenever you are."

"Thanks. I'll have her back in a bit."

"Take your time."

She led Beauty out of the barn before she mounted the mare and started them on their little sojourn.

Wayne Dunbar. What a curious surprise. In a time when she didn't think she had time for the whims of romance, there he popped up.

Far from her vision of what her lover would be, but he had been persistent enough for her to pay attention.

Her mom had spent the better part of her adult life alone and lonely, missing her father. It bothered her that the woman hadn't even seemed to try to find love again. *Was she trying to protect herself? Was she afraid of getting hurt?* Sometimes Desi had those fears. Fears of losing Wayne, fears of him leaving her. It wasn't anything he did, in fact all his actions pointed to him, for better or for worse, staying right by her side. Pursuing her, showering her with affection, professing his love, letting her know that he was there and planning to go nowhere.

That was beautiful, she thought, for sure. The entire thing was something she had never really thought was going to pan out for her the way it had. She was a skeptic, much like her rambunctious little pupil, Roy.

The corner of her mouth pulled up. She recalled for some reason the moment the little boy had professed how much he liked her as a teacher. She'd never thought Roy would be the one.

She laughed.

Then again, she hadn't thought Wayne would be either. But she knew without a shadow of a doubt that Wayne was her person. Only death could ever change that.

| 33 | My Cherry Pie |

Wayne walked up the few steps to Desiree's front porch and rang the bell.

It had been almost two weeks since he saw her in L.A. They had video chatted since then, of course, but nothin' was like the real thing. He had been pulled unexpectedly to Dallas and was putting in an obnoxious amount of hours training in preparation for the competition.

His chest tightened when she pulled the door open. She wiped her hands on her apron. Seeing her that way, barefoot in that damn stained apron, made the caveman in him want to grunt. Her coils were pulled back in a low puffy bun and a bonnet covered her head.

She laughed uncomfortably, bringing her eyes to her ensemble. "I know I look a mess. I was just on my way upstairs to—"

He couldn't restrain himself anymore. He pulled the beautiful woman into a warm embrace, eliciting a yelp from her. He pulled back just enough to gaze into her eyes and plant a sweet, chaste, kiss on her mouth.

She smirked up at him, her dainty fingers stroking his chest. "I missed you too."

"Really?" He pulled away and walked into the house toward the delicious smell. His nose never led him astray. He recalled his bout in the barrel when he first met her. The same floral scent filled her house too. It was light and pleasant. A billowing curtain brought his attention to an open window and right outside was a lilac bush.

He heard the front door close behind him. "Why does that sound so hard for you to believe?"

"You never really tell me you miss me. Sometimes you got me thinkin' that you kind of like all the time I'm away." He set his bottle of wine on the counter.

"Don't be silly. Of course I want to be in your arms every night."

He turned to face her when she breezed into the kitchen. The space was small which made her, standing at the stove, a close temptation. He cleared his throat. "That so?" He stuffed his hands in his pocket when his thoughts strayed to touching her again. "How're you doin'? You know, with your mom and stuff."

She glanced at him over her shoulder, her frown loosening. "Better." She exhaled and put the top back on the pot she was stirring. "Derrick seems to be taking it really hard, though. He was so stoic during the funeral. Like he always has to be the strong one, you know, ever since Pa died." She swallowed and pinched the bridge of her nose.

He couldn't stay away. He folded her into his arms, her back to his front, and she leaned back into him.

"I'm sorry I asked."

"Why?"

"I don't want to make you sad."

She turned to face him, staying in his hold. "I'm glad you asked." She cupped his cheek and he exhaled, relaxing for the first time now that he had her in his arms. She pushed up on her tiptoes and kissed him. He wanted to deepen the kiss, but his stomach betrayed him with a growl.

She laughed. "Food is pretty much ready. I, on the other hand—" She yipped when he grabbed her up again.

"You're perfect like this."

She laughed and pushed him away when he rubbed her neck with his facial hair. She squealed, making him laugh.

She started up the stairs. "I'll be back down in a minute."

He wanted to follow her, but he forced himself to stay put. When she was out of sight it was easier for him to think about...anything else. He walked around her living room and picked up a picture of her and her parents. She had pictures of her and family members, an older photo with her parents, on what looked like their wedding day.

He'd been in her house before, but he'd never paid much attention to the details. He wondered if he would make it into one of her frames. Out in the open and proud, born of a desire to see him every day, and of course, to smile when she did.

"Eileen and Harold Limb. Married August 17 on the banks of the Mississippi."

He smiled when he glanced over his shoulder and found his beautiful companion approaching him. She had put on a pretty little pink cotton dress and her hair was arranged in a tamed array of curls. Her hair was so dark it was like midnight. A simple silver necklace rested on her chest just above her breasts, hidden below the neckline of the garment.

He faced her, not caring about anything but her at the moment.

She extended her hand and waited until he took it. "We should eat while the food is hot. I heard your new salsa commercial on the radio."

He groaned, helping her plate the dishes.

"Salsa that's *raging* mad."

He laughed at her attempt at mocking his low voice. "That was pretty damn good."

"You don't have to lie to me."

"I would never. What we eatin'? Smells delicious."

She turned to face him, the gravy holder in her hand. "Smothered pork chops, mac 'n' cheese, greens, and hot water cornbread."

"God damn it, woman, you're about to put me a coma." The joy he felt in his chest spilled over into a Cheshire Cat smile.

She giggled. "Grab the plates, will you?"

"Of course, pretty lady."

"Dining room is through the other door." She pointed with her elbow.

As expected, dinner was delicious. He was now out on the back side of her wrap around porch in a mild food coma looking up at the stars. That was where he had held her the morning after she cried over her mother's death.

He loved the porch. It was just perfect.

"Here you go." She handed him the cherry pie a la mode and his mouth started to water. He took a deep breath making room for desert. Wasn't no chance in hell he was going to say to no to pie.

"Aww boy, I do love me a good ol' pie. The rest of 'em can keep their dry old cakes. Pie for me any day of the week."

She laughed, sitting next to him with a plate of her own.

He frowned. "Where's your ice cream?"

She frowned back. "Not really a fan."

"WHAT!" He was truly shocked, so much so that he leaned forward to put his plate down. He had to get to the bottom of this because it made no sense to him. "How could you not like ice cream?"

She shrugged and took a mouth full of pie. A rogue cherry fell right between her breasts. All of the excitement he had for the pending conversation about the unequivocal delight of ice cream rushed down to his pants.

"Oh shit," she mumbled. He grabbed her hand before she reached down there to retrieve it. "Wayne—" Her words stopped in her throat when she met his determined gaze. He took her pie plate and set it down on the coffee table next to his own.

He grabbed the neckline of her dress and carefully pulled it down under her bra. His insides twisted in anticipation and his heartbeat sped up in his chest, pumping blood where it belonged.

He smirked when he saw the delicious crumbs sitting under the trail of cherry juice and nestled between her generous breasts. He wiped up the cherry juice trail with his pointer finger and licked the confection off his digit. "Mmm," he moaned. Graham cracker crust. His favorite.

"Wayne—" He put that same finger over her mouth and held her eyes for a moment. He picked up more of the juice and traced her bottom lip with it.

"Uh-uh," he warned when her tongue stuck out of her mouth. "That's mine."

Hmm, he thought, examining the front-clasp bra. It didn't take him but a moment to figure out how to open it, gently though, careful not to lose the sweet dessert. He ran his tongue between her breast from the bottom up until the cherry fell into his open mouth. "Fuck, that's good."

Her chest was rising and falling in staggered breaths, an obvious struggle.

He clasped her neck, angling her face up to meet his. His other hand pinched her nipple. She moaned and arched toward him, making him grow harder in his pants. It was painful, literally.

He licked her bottom lip, tasting the cherries, yes, but tasting her. He missed her. He missed being around her, feeling her presence, tasting her mouth. He pressed their mouths together. The kiss became more urgent with that familiar heat of need, of want, of play, of being deep inside her. The hand toying with her nipple dipped between her legs and she opened them shamelessly, without question or argument.

Yes, he thought.

Mine.

My sweet flower.

Open for me.

| 34 | Pretty Miss Limb |

Wayne flexed his hips and moaned when he felt something warm and wet wrap around his penis. His groggy mind was struggling to figure out what exactly was going on, but his body seemed to know exactly what was needed. Blood started flowing to the growing anatomy before another moan slipped from his lips. His finger encountered thick coiled hair. It wasn't long before he located the neck the hair belonged to.

His beautiful temptress laughed as she licked up his length and guided her mouth back down. Her hand was wrapped around him as well, gripping him firmly and moving the skin up and down steadily while her tongue suckled the tip.

"Mmm, that's how I want you," she moaned, sitting up. One of his eyes opened when the bed shifted. She was reaching over him, her naked perfection grazing over his chest as she grabbed a condom from the bedside table.

His heavy eyelids fell open when she rolled the condom over him. She straddled him and he gripped her thighs, running his hands up to cradle her ass.

Yes, that was his ass. So soft, so lush. She grabbed him and aligned him with her sex before she slowly took him in.

His mouth opened even as his eyes stayed closed. Not that he didn't want to see her, it was that sleep still clinging to his brain. As much as it all felt real, he wouldn't be surprised if he woke up to find it was all his own imagination.

"Aww, fuck, Desi you're so—" He clenched his teeth when she pulled up his length and let her weight fall. His arms were too weak to hold her. She leaned down and kissed him while rocking her body over his.

Though slow to start, it didn't take much time for him to wake up enough to increase the pace of their encounter. He thrusted his hips in rapid succession, yielding moaning screams from her. He held her ass in place and penetrated her over and over through her pleading moans. He felt her pussy swell and tighten around him. He felt her getting close. He'd released only hours before, so it wasn't a priority at the moment. She should have left him sleeping if she thought she was getting out of this without coming.

He flipped her on her side and pulled her ass back toward him to slide in from behind. He kissed her shoulder and held her body close to his, thrusting with purpose, slower, deeper. He let his finger find her clit and she let out a strained gasp.

"Is this why you woke me up?" he whispered in her ear before he took the sensitive skin between his lips. He moaned in her ear, feeling her body move back against him.

"Wayne, please."

"Uh-uh. You should have left me sleeping. Now I want to feel you come."

She moaned, pants escaping her mouth. She moaned again when he pinched a nipple. Her clit swelled with his consistent strokes. Her movements became jerky then faltered and she trembled in his arms.

"Fuck," he said, feeling her pussy grip him over and over in her release.

*

His hearing came first. The sound of birds chirping.

One eye opened to a bright window in front of him. He shielded the light as his eyes adjusted. He frowned when he saw lacy curtains. He inhaled and finally his mind placed where he was.

He took account of all his faculties. He was sore, but he felt damn good. Vibrant and—

160

His thought drifted when he felt next to him and found the other side of the bed empty. He sat up and looked around.

The woman was nowhere to be found. His train of thought shifted and his stomach growled when he smelled bacon.

"Aww fuck." If his sweet siren was cooking right now he was going to lose all his home training. He tossed his legs over the side of the bed and yawned with a stretch. Who the hell was he foolin'? He didn't have no home trainin'.

Before he headed downstairs he peed and brushed his teeth, mostly because she refused to kiss him in the mornin' if he didn't. He learned that the hard way.

He exhaled when he stepped off the last step and looked toward the kitchen to see Desi working diligently at the stove. He smiled when he found her wearing his shirt while she worked. He had been wondering where it had gone, but he didn't want it anywhere other than where it was.

"You mind setting the table?" she said without looking at him.

He strolled up to her, slipped his arms around her and pressed a kiss to her neck. She looked back at him, tilting her head. He'd been spoiled the past week. Ever since she had cooked a whole damn meal for him, with a cherry pie on top, he'd been over there getting spoiled rotten all week.

It started with a cup of coffee in the morning. By the time he'd wake up she was out of the house early to get to school. He was in practices until evening and would come over to find a meal waitin' for him.

Felt easy, the whole exchange, a delightful preview of what his future would be like.

"Mornin', darlin'." He leaned down and kissed her lips. It was Saturday, the big day.

"Good morning." She said when he finally pulled away.

He reluctantly let her go and retrieved the place mats and silverware and set the table. Then got the paper and brought it inside while she put the plates together. He grabbed the plates off the counter and she got the orange juice.

"Coffee?"

He shook his head. He didn't like drinking coffee on rodeo days. Made him jittery.

She sat down and he pushed in her chair then took his seat in the spot next to her. "Thanks for breakfast—" He frowned down at his plate and looked up at her as she opened the paper to International Business, her favorite section. "Honey, where's my bacon?"

She folded down a corner of the paper. "It's in the omelet."

He smiled.

"You know, so you won't taste the vegetables." She added adjusting the paper.

He nodded. How did she know him so well after only a week? He didn't complain when she cooked. If she set it in front of him, he'd eat it. He liked that she had a garden. It made the vegetables more bearable.

"I like your vegetables, babe."

"Mhm," she said. "You want the local news?"

"You know it."

They ate in silence, reading their paper, talking here and there about the things they read that were of interest.

When he was done, he wiped his mouth and sat back, closing his paper and setting it on the table. He looked out the window at the back yard. He could see the garden and other landscaping.

He smiled.

He looked up at Desi when she went to grab his plate. "I'll get the dishes."

"It's okay. I have a whole list of other things that I need you to do."

He perked up at this and scrambled to his feet, helping her clear the table.

"The front screen door needs oiling, two light bulbs in the bathroom need changing, and I need you to make sure none of the screens on the porch have holes in the netting."

He pulled her into his arms while she stood rinsing the dishes at the sink. "Yes ma'am," he said, pressing a kiss to her neck.

She let her head fall back to look at him. "Thank you." She puckered her lips and he kissed her, then pulled away to do what she asked of him.

This was the best way to spend the morning of a big competition, just doing some small menial tasks. Helped keep his mind off the anxious things and kept his hands busy, his mind busy. It also felt good to be needed by his woman.

By the time he was done with his tasks, he was ready to start getting ready for the showdown.

| 35 | Flower & Rage |

"Des! I'm headin' out!" Wayne yelled up the stairs. He grabbed up his bags, which were waitin' by the door.

Strong grip, loose hips, settle on straight. Be agile and ready to roll into the first buck. He opened the door, smiling when the screen didn't squeak. He was already dressed in his jeans, shirt and boots.

"Hey cowboy."

The corner of his mouth lifted and he glanced over his shoulder to find his sexy little lady dressed in an all-black outfit with tassles on the sleeves of her jacket with a red dress shirt underneath.

He frowned when he saw his old tattered brown hat on her head. "Think you're forgetting something."

"You sure as hell are right I am." It took two strides for him to get the woman in his arms. She giggled and put the hat on his head before he leaned down and kissed her. She held his head by the back of his neck and he angled his face over hers.

He kissed her neck and she leaned back against the door frame and let her head fall to the side. He kissed down the long column of her neck, heat racing through his body. His heartbeat picked up. He wanted this woman.

He unbuckled her jeans and pushed them over her hips.

"You're going to be late."

"I got time." That was kind of a lie, but he'd always make time to have her. He brought himself to his knees. He lifted her leg to rest on his shoulder. He rubbed his thumb over her pussy through her panties. She moaned and leaned her back against the doorframe.

"Wayne," she whimpered when he pushed her panties aside and slid a finger inside her. His gaze was intently focused on her sex, his eyebrows pulled together while he worked her diligently. She needed to lean on the door for support.

Her breath caught when his mouth closed around her swollen clitoris. She pulled her fingers through his hair and gripped his strands tight. Forcing rolls of heat through his body.

She rotated her hips while he pressed her to his face with a large hand squeezing her ass. Yes! He thought enthralled in the moment, the feel of her reaction to him, her desire, his growing need. He moved his face back and forth over her pussy and teased her G-spot with his free hand with one intention, to coax her to completion. He felt her heat up under him her moans were staggered and airy.

A shiver was only the beginning, followed by a throbbing pressure around his finger. Her head fell back, mouth open with a great cry when the orgasm seized through her body.

He pulled away with a look of complete satisfaction. As much as he wanted to satiate his own lust, he was going to be late. Late for what? Good question considering he was the show.

He kissed her lips before placing his hat back on his head and heading out the screen door.

*

It felt like only moments had passed since he'd kissed his Desi goodbye. He rotated his shoulders and flexed his hand.

The grip was coming back ever since his Desi had started massaging essential oils into his hand again. He gripped the rope wrapped around the big angry animal between his legs. He heard the beast blow air through his nose.

Strong grip, loose hips, settle on straight. Be agile and ready to roll into the first buck.

Rage wasn't just any bull. The stands were to full capacity, so full they actually ran out of tickets. The most anticipated event hyped up on radio and television commercials, interviews, and something called memes. Rage versus Wayne. He patted the bull on the side.

He gave the signal and they opened the gate.

The familiar rush of adrenaline pushed through him the first time the bull bucked. He let his body roll with the bull's and back down. Just another second. He tried to dislodge his hand, but he had wrapped it too tight in the ropes. He started falling off, but his hand was still trapped. He screamed out in pain when he felt his arm get yanked in another direction.

Wayne flung loose from the bull, but as he flopped onto the ground the large animal had its anger set on Wayne. He scrambled to his feet but before he could get away, he felt the large animal's head lift him in the air and toss him somewhere. The wind flew from his lungs. Despite the fact that he knew he had to get up, his limbs were laden and he couldn't move. He no longer heard the audience, he just heard his own blood rushing to his heart. He looked up, but his vision was blurred with blood. He touched his head even as bodies passed him. He tried to get up, but he kept falling back to the ground. He glanced back after wiping away the blood to find the pen littered with clowns limping away. He didn't have to ask to know they were victims of the two-ton menice. Rage had his gaze focused back on Wayne. The idiot who thought this show was about him.

The bull blew out air from his large nostrils and kicked back his hoofs. Wayne turned on his stomach and stumbled to his feet but kept falling. Before he could start limping toward the exit in an attempt to escape, the audience's gasp brought his attention, and Rage's, to a bright red floating scarf.

No! His chest felt like it was squeezing in on itself as Desi stood with her head down in the middle of the ring. It looked like some Vegas performance how she stood there with the red cloth taken by the wind. She was wearing the all black outfit with the tassled sleeves.

Rage turned, his attention diverted. He lined up with Desi instead, who still stood there patiently. Her black hat with studs was the only thing anyone could see, but Wayne knew her figure and the outfit he had peeled her out of only a few hours before.

When he got to his feet, instead of running to get out of the pen like he should have done, he ran toward her. The bull was charging at the same time; he wasn't sure if he'd make it.

He shoved her out of the way just before the bull's massive head scooped him up and flung him like a rag doll across the pen. The sickening crunch of his arm when he hit the dirt ricocheted through his body with a searing pain.

He thought about getting up, but he wobbled back to his knees.

Desi, he thought. He fell on a heap of broken wood; he had no idea where it had come from. He thought he was looking around, but the world was spinning and nothing made sense.

Desi. Where was she?

The pain in his arm was so much that his world started to blur a bit. He felt wetness on his cheek, so he touched it and pulled away with blood.

Damn, he thought before he fell on his back. He was staring up at the sky then darkness then the sky again. Time meant nothing to him.

He tried to look around to find her, but they kept forcing him to look into the damn light.

Desi, his mind whispered before he faded.

| 36 | Wayne & Rage |

Desi settled next to Aubrey, packed tight. The audience was so thick it was insane. They usually had a good turnout, but nothing like that. The crowd had just stopped cheering at another bull running into the corral.

"I didn't miss him, did I?"

Aubrey laughed, scooting over as much as she could and handing over the concession goodies. "No. Whoa, girl, you're really embracing the sponsored theme, huh?"

She laughed. "Oh yeah. I'm a raving fan now that my *boyfriend* is competing." She wasn't used to being late, but her last minute rendezvous with Wayne left her needing to get ready for a second time.

Aubrey laughed. "Good to know you're finally claiming the man, even though the whole city already knew."

Desi giggled, munching on a nacho chip. "No, the whole city *speculated*. Totally different."

"Now, the moment we've all been waiting for," the announcer said, getting the crowd to quiet down. Even in the hushed silence the energy was live, thick with excitement and speculation. "Rrrrrraaaaaggggeeeeeee and Waaaaayyynnnneee!" The crowd erupted in cheers and most of them shot to their feet, including Desi and Aubrey.

There he was, perched on top of the large animal in the small little pen. They had pretty close seats, but not good enough to see the set look on his face. She knew that look though, determined, focused, the same way he had looked a few moments before when he was determined to make her feel his desire.

He had dashed out the door before she had a chance to have him the way she really wanted him—

She broke from her rather lucid and massively inappropriate thoughts when the pen door flew open and out came the bucking, angry bull. She'd seen her share of rodeos, most people had, but this bull was just ornery.

Wayne flowed with the big animal's bucks. The crowd started counting down until they blew up in cheers once the time he needed passed.

She frowned when he started sliding off.

"Get off the damn bull," she whispered under her breath. "You have nothing to prove. Get the hell off!" His legs were on the ground, trying to keep up with the animal, which became more determined to exact revenge on the human still attached. Something was wrong. "Something's wrong. SOMETHING'S WRONG!" she shouted, but no one could hear her over all the noise.

The announcer was rambling on and people were cheering for God's knows what. They just wanted a show.

She didn't notice that she was pressed against the railing at the bottom of the stairs. The audience cheered louder, looking away from the pen. Her breath caught in her chest when she saw Wayne land on the hard ground. He moved, but slowly, and his arm laid in a strange position.

She looked around, trying to figure out what to do. She hopped over the railing then climbed the pen wall and perched there as several clowns ran into the pen. The bull caught them one by one with his horns. One got under his hoof. He charged, smashing through a barrel and catching another clown who was inside the barrel with his horn.

Shit!

She closed her eyes and looked away. He was on a rampage and he wouldn't stop until he got—

Her breath caught when Wayne got to his feet and staggered toward the gate. His legs kept giving out for some reason. Rage lined up with the man, blowing out air from his nostrils. She knew this move and at the rate the bull was going there was only one way this was going to go. She hopped off the pen wall into the dirt circle and walked up to the center of the circle. She pulled the red scarf away from her neck and held it up.

The audience went silent. She looked up from under the rim of the hat and saw the bull's attention on her. Good. She hoped Wayne would use the moment to get to safety.

The bull lined up again, focused on her this time. She held the handkerchief out to the side. He puffed air out his nose and kicked his legs back before he started charging toward her.

Closer, closer. She took a deep breath. Closer. She bent her legs a little set to move aside when something plowed into her that wasn't the bull, sending her flying. It was as solid as a bull might be, but that could have also been the speed. She rolled in the dirt, struggling to get up onto her stomach. She heard a loud crash. She looked toward the sound and found Wayne sprawled out with a barrel's worth of splintered wood around him.

He wasn't moving and her heart flew into her chest.

Was he hurt? Was he unconscious? Why wasn't he moving? That was part of the training. *Get up. No matter what.*

She looked behind her and found the animal circling to find its next target. She frowned, pissed all the way off. She caught a glimpse of Wayne moving a little bit, but not much. The medical personnel were waiting right outside the pen for safety's sake. She had to get this over with quickly. She took off her black coat now, the red shirt creating the target that she wanted. The bull had sure earned his name with the crazy anger in his eyes. She moved slowly, looking over her shoulder, making sure his corral was right behind her.

She stood there waiting as the bull started charging at her, faster and faster, picking up speed.

Wait, not yet.

Wait, not yet.

She dove to the side like she'd done many times before and felt the intense rush of air blowing past her. For the first time in who knew how long, she heard the crowd again erupt in cheers and applause. The medical staff rushed in to help Wayne and some of the wounded clowns.

"You saw it, ladies and gentlemen! The match of the century between not only Rage and Wayne, but Rage and the Mad Matador!"

| 37 | Rage's Aftermath |

Wayne's body was like lead. The parts he could feel, anyway. He tried to move his toe, but there was a brick holding it still. His lids lifted with much effort and he groaned at the bright lights all around him.

He felt a warm hand on his bare arm. "Easy."

His insides smiled before his mouth mustered up the effort.

He knew that voice.

He felt something on his face and he reached for it, but his hand was pulled away.

"I called the doctor. Just, try not to touch anything."

"Are you hurt?" He didn't recognize the croaking, cracking voice. Sounded like he was going through puberty. That's when he realized he was thirsty. "Water."

"The doctor will be here soon."

He managed to get his eyes open again and held the pretty woman in his sight. "Did he hurt you?"

"I'm fine." Tears started to well up in her eyes. "I'm sorry you're hurt."

She grabbed his hand when he tried to reach for her. He leaned into her other hand that rested against his face. His eyes closed and he revelled in the gentle warmth of her soft palms on his cheek.

Her signature scent filled him up from the inside recalling all the things that had happened over the past several months. Eventually his recollection settled on the last day he remembered.

It started off beyond amazing, a glimpse into a wonderful life with his girl.

He frowned when he zeroed in on the madness that was Wayne versus Rage.

The damn beast had tossed him about real good. He was struggling to get his footing right. He looked back to see where the angry animal was only to find standing in the middle of the dirt ring was his Desi.

There was a kaleidoscope of emotions that floated through him, all tore up in the hospital with half his body wrapped up, with tubes running in and out of him. He focused on one of those emotions, unable to process the others: anger.

"Why the hell were you in that pen?" His brows were pulled together when he met the woman's confused facial expression.

Had he studdard?

"Wayne this isn't the—"

"Naw. Of all the things I was to be worryin' over, you weren't supposed to be one of 'em."

She exhaled and fixed her mouth to say something, but he wasn't done yet.

"Wasn't me that agreed to keep my ass on the side lines. Wasn't me that promised I wouldn't get in the damn pen again."

"Wayne—"

"Ain't done yet." He coughed a little bit, but was determined to speak his mind. "You knew what it did to me seein' you in that pen playin' with death. You - you promised. You. You did that. You agreed you wouldn't do it that you didn't need to. I took care of everything. Every reason that put you in that pen I covered it."

She rolled her eyes. "What, to lord it over me?"

"NO woman! Don't you get it?" He coughed. "To make you feel safe. Lettin' you know you're not in it alone. You got someone. The hell were you thinkin', Des?"

She crossed her arms over her chest and raised an eyebrow.

"Well? Got anything to say for yourself?" He looked at her with an accusatory snarl.

"Are you going to actually let me talk?"

He winced when he tried to shrug. "Don't make no never mind anyways. If you're going to continue to break your own daggum promises, the hell we going—"

"Alright Mr. Dunbar." The doctor breezed into the room with Wayne's chart in his hands. "Well, let's see. Seems like we've got some good news and some bad news. Which would you like to hear first?"

"Good news." He needed something positive in his moment of pain.

"The surgery went off without a hitch and you'll have a full recovery, I'd wager."

"What's so bad after that?"

"It's going to take time and proper care. Absolutely no riding, consistent physical therapy, the whole nine yards for everything to get back on track. You might even be out for an entire season. Or, out permanently."

He grumbled. That was bad news. *What the hell am I going to do without bull riding?*

"Shall we go down the list? We've got an arm broken in two places, sprained wrist and broken pinky on that same side. I'd say you're lucky considering what happened. Most of what you're feeling are just bumps and bruises. You'll heal out of those in a couple weeks. At any rate, we have you on a robust pain management plan, so you should be—"

"No."

The doctor frowned. "Excuse me?"

"No medication, except for Tylenol or something."

"Wayne!" Desi said, frowning down at him.

"Mr. Dunbar, there is no need to be in pain," the doctor said.

"You heal faster without 'em don't you?"

The doctor frowned. "There has been evidence in some studies, but it's not a guarantee—"

"That's what I want."

174

The doctor exhaled and frowned. "It's going to be beyond discomfort, at least for the first few weeks."

He nodded. "I can handle it." A painful arm sounded more appealing than layin' up somewhere for weeks feeling numb.

"Very well then." The doctor walked over to the IV. "We should start while you're still in the hospital so we can determine if this is really the way you want to go."

"Fair enough, doc. Hey, could I get some water?"

"Sure, I'll send in a nurse."

The air was thick once the doctor left. Heavy from the news, heavy from the previous conversation.

"I might have to step out. I'm expecting a call from Derrick."

"What for?"

She frowned, leaning on the wall near the door. Her arms were crossed over her chest and she looked irritated. Tired and irritated. He cared more than he wanted to. He had to hold firm because he didn't want her thinkin' she was always going to get her way even if she was wrong.

"I don't need a reason to talk to my brother."

He snapped into the present moment. "Ain't say you did."

She exhaled and ran her hand down her face. "We're planning to clean out my mom's house soon. Look..." She pushed off the wall and wandered toward the bed, but she didn't get as close as she was before.

She took a deep breath before she spoke. He could see in that moment how exhausted she was and his chest pressed against his rib cage. "There's really no good time to tell you this, but I'd rather you hear it from me."

It was his turn to release a deep exhale. "What's that?"

She looked up at him from under her lashes. "I started clowning for some extra cash, yes. But the truth is, I really love it."

His jaw clenched everything he could feel gripping onto itself. She was right he wasn't going to like this one bit now was he?

"Desi—"

"I know how you feel about it and after everything that happened, I understand why it bothers you so much but—"

175

"No! You don't understand! How the hell could you!"

"Wayne—

"NO!" He cleared his dry throat irritated by him raising his voice.

"You haven't even heard me out!"

"Don't need to!" He coughed wishing he had that water.

Silence sat there for a moment, charged like it was electricity rumbling away in a cloud. Hot and tense they stared each other down. He wasn't going to back off this one. He'd rolled over for every little thing concernin' the woman but this, he couldn't.

"I-I think I found a way for both of us to get what we want."

He grumbled and leaned against the pillow focused on the ceiling. There wasn't really anything that could make him change how he felt about it. She did it for the money, he made it so she didn't need no money. It seemed a simple equation to him and he wasn't the brightest bulb for sure.

She must have taken his silence as a cue to keep talking.

"I was approached by the man who owns the stadium and he wants me to train a special group of clowning matadors to put on a little show. People seemed to love it. I mean, the media's been eating the entire thing up."

"No. I don't like the idea of—"

"Well I do!"

"FINE!" He felt the heat of anger rush through him. "If you've already got your mind made up, then what the hell you doin' here then?" If he could cross his arms and pout, he would, but he couldn't. Everything that wasn't in a sling or cast hurt too bad.

"You should—"

"DON'T YOU TELL MY ASS WHAT I SHOULD DO!"

She pinched her nose. "Wayne—" She trailed off and looked down at her phone with a deep frown. Her delicate brows creased briefly. "It's Derrick. I have to get it."

"Des—"

"Sorry," she held a finger in his direction answering the call. That got his blood boilin'. He was in no state to be put on hold. He might should have been less confrontational, but he couldn't find it right then.

"We ain't done talkin', Not by a long shot." He yelled as she headed to the door.

She covered the phone's speaker and addressed him over her shoulder. "We're done talking about the gig. It's my life. I'm doing it. We can talk about everything else when I get back. Hopefully then you'll have calmed down." She hurried out of the room with the phone against her ear. "What you say Dare? Hard time hearing you. I'm at the hospital—"

Oh boy, was he steamin' hot mad at his lady and he ain't ever felt so hot at anyone before.

What the hell kind of partnership was this anyway? She obviously didn't care what he wanted or what he thought. It was all about Desi and what she wanted which he wouldn't mind too much accept she was puttin' herself in danger. Besides that, she put him on pause. That, to him, was just disrespectful no matter the circumstances.

"You're a pigheaded pansy, you know that?" Wayne frowned first, then smirked when he saw his sister leaning in the doorway. She pushed off the door frame and strolled into the room to stand next to her brother's bed.

"Hello to you too, Joey Lou."

"Look at you. Goddamn Wayne you look like a truck done run you over."

"Gee thanks. Always count on you for a self esteem boost." He closed his eyes and leaned against the pillow.

She laughed. "All for what? That girl? Same one that was actin' like your wife or somethin'? Doctors are all going up to her for decisions on what to do with you. Askin' her all sorts of questions about you."

"They were?"

"Yeah, I set 'em straight though."

He frowned.

My wife.

The thought wouldn't stray far from his mind even being blazin' mad it wouldn't.

He'd thought maybe one day he'd settle down, wife and kids and all that. But it seemed to be more someone else's dream than any reality he ever wanted.

He brought his attention back to his sibling when her words finally settled into his mind. "What'd you mean you set 'em straight?"

"Told 'em the truth, that she wasn't the decision maker, and she wasn't even family."

"Joey Lou," he scolded the woman, who was a spitting image of their father, save for the gender thing.

"What? You know what this means? You're ruined. You're going to lose all them fancy contracts—"

"We're not talkin' about this right now. What happened didn't have nothin' to do with Desi."

"Tellin' me you'd've done what you did for one of them other buffoons? Men get messed up toyin' with them bulls like that." The woman wiped away angry tears.

His frustration softened. He wasn't sure when the last time was he'd seen his sister cry.

"Come on Joey Lou. It's—"

"Mom died, dad too. You wanna be next? Or just paralyzed head to toe so you can't do anything for yourself. Who do you think is going to be wipin' your ass? Desi?" She said Desi's name with such distaste that he looked away. "ME! It'll be me, and I'll do it. Won't complain of course, not one bit, because I'm your family. Ya hear me? ME! I'm all you got! These chicks been walkin' in an out since you're in high school. When she walks on out, I'mma be what you got left."

He looked back at his sister. She was a flushed mess of sadness and frustration. That was one thing about Joey Lou, she held stuff in like a kettle filled with water. All it took was some heat and she'd eventually bubble over.

He took her hand with his good one and held it. "Yeah, I hear you." He didn't want to though. He didn't want to hear that his beautiful bull-teasing rosebud wouldn't be by his side to wipe his ass if need be or have him wipe hers. She left him once, when things got dicey, would she do it again?

His sister pulled the extra blanket up to his chest and perched on the bed. "Where the hell is that doggone nurse with that water?" She fumbled with the edge of the blanket, tucking it in at his sides, smoothing it out, plumping his pillow. "You look like hell, you do. Just a slop bucket of a mess."

| 38 | Wayne is Such a Lonely Number |

Wayne grumbled when he read Desi's last message from three days ago. He wiggled his fingers over the phone debating with himself, before he placed it face down on the table. He'd been reading it and rereading it, typing a message or ten then erasing them.

He refused to respond to it. If she thought she was going to tell him when he was done talking about something, then he wasn't going to say anything at all.

He was pulled from his thoughts when he heard the screen door open. Yep, he was home. He'd been home for the past several weeks ever since he was finally released from the hospital.

"Hello, Wayne? You here?"

His chest fell back into his person and he choked down hope which was quickly replaced with irritation. "Kyle." He said the man's name blandly.

"Good to see you too, Wayne." Kyle said pushing up the glasses on his face. "Since you're in such a good mood, I'll keep things short." He breezed into the house tucking his car keys into his pocket and setting his briefcase on the coffee table. Wayne perched on the edge of the chair across from the couch.

He wasn't in the mood to sit, neither was he in the mood to stand. He tried to scratch his arm under the cast, then got irritated because he couldn't reach it like he wanted. He was grateful the damn thing would be coming off in a couple days. Almost six weeks since the incident and he was beyond restless. To compound it all, he hadn't talked to Desi either, well, not directly anyway, since their blow up in the hospital.

"So, Elizabeth has an endless pile of media outlets that want to interview you."

Wayne grumbled. He'd been trashing all the requests for interviews ever since Kyle first brought them to the table. Damn vultures flooded him with requests before he was even out of the hospital.

"I picked out the five I thought might be the best."

"I don't wanna do it. Same as I said last time you were here. Same I'mma say next time I see you." He slouched against the back of the chair.

"I hear you, but I think you should at least consider it. I think you'd be surprised at what you get."

"Besides a trip down memory lane, that I don't wanna go down, ain't sure I care to know."

Kyle frowned. "Your fans love you. I mean you look like hell, but you beat your time, no one could even get close to the time you stayed on the epic Rage. Not to mention all the new very enthusiastic female fans you have since saving Desi—"

"We both know I ain't save her."

The man shrugged. "They don't seem to care, and neither should you, man come on. You're in the prime of your career."

He grumbled and pushed to his feet. "Yeah, and I'm all busted up stuck in the damn house."

Kyle exhaled loading all the paperwork back in his briefcase. "You wouldn't be if you'd stop trying to avoid everybody." He stood up. "Guess I should just get to why you really wanted me to come over then, huh?"

Wayne glanced back at the man over his shoulder annoyed at how interested he was in what news, if any, he had about Des.

"The only thing I heard from Desi is that her plans to return are delayed."

"Did she say when she was coming back?"

"If you want more information, you'll have to reach out to her." Kyle headed toward the door with Wayne not too far behind.

"Oh come on Kyle, you gotta know more. How did she sound? Did you talk to her? Is she alright out in Houston? Does she need anything, money, movers, people to handle the estate auction?"

Kyle stopped and turned to look at Wayne with the door open on his car. "Like I said, if you want more information, you'll have to get it yourself. Messenger pigeon signing off." The man frowned and paused before he sat in the driver side seat. "If I had to guess, I'd say this is the hardest part of her life. Look, I don't know what transpired between you two, but I doubt it's worth all this. Good luck at the doctor's office. I'll see you next week, same time."

"Yeah, yeah same time." Wayne mumbled leaning on the open door with his mind churning. He hated feeling the way he did mostly because he had no idea what to do with it.

He remembered at that moment why he stayed single for the majority of his adult life.

He didn't want to go back inside so he headed down to the barn. He saw Joey Lou disappear that way an hour or so ago, maybe she needed help with somethin'.

"Would you stop that? I got this," Joey Lou said, with all the frustration of someone who had had way more than enough of him.

"This arm is perfectly fine," he barked, knowing good and well he was being a nuisance just to keep his mind off things. It'd been barely thirty minutes since Kyle left with his update, and Wayne'd been in his mind ever since.

"Go sit your ole busted ass down and let me handle things."

He leaned the rake on the wall, breathing through the exhaustion. He'd been layin' around for weeks unable to get out and his stamina had suffered because of it.

"Shoulda taken that good pain killer. Even if you didn't want it, I could have sold that. I know some house moms in the burbs who'd've liked that medical grade stuff."

Wayne rolled his eyes and leaned on the opening to the barn. "Since when did you become a drug pusher?"

"Thanks to you? Never, 'cause you always gotta handle things on your own." She raked out the stall she was working on and stood straight, leaning on the rake. "You're dumb as two left shoes, ya know. Standin' there in pain when you could be relaxin' in the house with a coke or beer."

"I'm tired of bein' in the house." He sounded more like one of Desi's elementary age children, but he felt worse.

"Tired of bein' in your head more like," she mumbled under her breath.

He frowned. "What do you mean?" He could tell his sister had been getting more and more frustrated lookin' after him as time went by, but he was so in his own shit he hadn't bothered to inquire after her until now.

"I see you," she said on exhale. "Moping about like the doctor said you only had a month left to live. I think we both know that arm'll heal, might take some time, but it will."

"Yeah, I know, but in the meantime I need somethin' to keep me busy."

"No, what you need to do is call that damn woman, Desi." She mentioned the other woman with a twinge of irritation in her voice. "You do that whole macho thing Dad used to do, 'cept she ain't mom."

"What you sayin' Joey Lou?"

"Sayin' that, you think you're tough by not going to see her, when all you're doin' is makin' both us miserable."

He raised an eyebrow. "Not used to you being such a deep thinker."

She looked away, but not before he could see her cheeks flush. "Been takin' classes at the school I clean toilets at. Don't have the money to pay for 'em, but the professor doesn't seem to mind me sitting in the back."

"School? Well, if you want to go to school, why didn't you say nothin'? I've got money oozin' out my ass, Joey Lou."

"Yeah, but that's your money."

He frowned, restraining the desire to scream at the girl. "Our money. It's ours. I didn't forget what I told Mom and Dad."

She tossed him a slight smile then shrugged. "Even with all the money, I wouldn't be able to school there no ways."

"What do you mean? You always kept your grades up."

She shrugged, focusing on adding fresh hay to the stall she was working in. "Yeah, but I ain't got no credentials—" She broke off when she noticed him closing in on her.

The corner of his mouth lifted into a rogue's smile. "You don't need all that. You got me."

She waved him off and stood up straight. "You goin' to the rodeo next friday?"

He grumbled. "I'd rather not watch what I should be doin'."

"You should go."

He frowned and leaned his weight on one leg. "That so? Why?"

"I heard some weird halftime show was meant to be happenin' at the stadium that night." She leaned her weight on the rake. "They callin' the performer The Mad Matador."

He frowned recalling his last conversation with Des. A floating joy moved around his chest. "You're keepin' tabs on Desi?"

She shrugged. "I ain't give no names."

"Joey Lou. I thought you didn't like her?"

She shrugged again. "She's not my girlfriend. I don't have to like her."

"That ain't altogether true now is it? There's gotta be somethin' you like, or you wouldn't waste your time."

"Alright, alright. If sayin' it will get you the hell out of this damn barn." She took a deep breath. "Don't get me wrong, because she was annoying as all hell that one with her questions, and monitoring every little damn thing they put you on." She exhaled. "Had to admit though by the end, I was grateful to have her there. Things I wouldn't have asked. Answerin' questions I ain't know the first thing on how to answer." She wiped the tears away smearing dirt on her face. "Just grateful someone was there, you know."

He pulled his sister into a hug that obviously caught the woman off guard. His Desi was lookin' after him. She had lots of practice with medical personnel with all that was going on with her mother the few months before the woman passed.

She held him for a long while before she finally pushed him away. "Alright, alright," she said finally. "I'm going to break out in hives if you keep with all the huggin'."

Wayne pulled away, holding her shoulder with his good arm. "You know, you're not so bad, Joey Lou."

She grumbled under her breath. "You should take a real shower."

He frowned. "Hell you sayin'?" He sniffed his armpit.

"Do I have to spell it out for ya?"

He snarled at her mostly because she was right. Moping around the house wallowing in his own self pity and mountains of pain was nothing compared to the wrenching of his soul being away from Desi. He was still upset with her for a number of things. Unresolved things that set festering while he set, laid, and lounged rotting away in his house.

He was under the water. Well, all of him except the arm that was in the cast. Awkward as all hell, but Joey Lou was right. He needed the shower.

To no surprise his thoughts settled on his woman. She seemed to do what she pleased from start to finish that one. Stubborn as she could be. Insisting on being in danger. He knew how to be the one in danger, but he didn't know how to play the other role. He never thought about how she might feel seeing him in danger every other week.

He had never thought about how she felt seeing him in the hospital, then being forced to make decisions about his well-being. From Joey Lou's description, it seemed like Desi was steppin' up and handling things that needed handlin'. Handling things with a focused fierceness that only his Desi could pull off. Lookin' after him when he wasn't able to look after himself. Lookin' after him like a true partner, like a—

Like a wife.

My wife.

Joey Lou's words whispered past his mind again like a flower petal on a breeze: '...actin' like your wife or somethin'.' That's what she said back in the hospital about Desi.

Maybe, just maybe, once they ironed out the things that needed straightenin', it was time for her to stop actin'.

| 39 | A Pie For Peace |

"What're you doin' here?" the knock-kneed woman asked, wiping her hands on her messy apron.

"Brought a pie." Desi presented a smile that she didn't even believe. She didn't feel like smiling. Not until she saw Wayne. Not until she could hold him in her arms.

He'd been ignoring her mostly. Sending updates through Kyle like a messenger pigeon and she knew why. She'd been so focused on the Matador thing and on what she wanted and how much she loved clownin' and stuntin', that she didn't care to even hear the man out. She made up her mind before they could even talk it over. In fact, in her mind there was nothing to talk over. Her time away, and being ignored, she saw the error of her aways. She didn't want Wayne Lording over her; so she couldn't do it to him.

She'd been so determined to do the Matador thing with or without Wayne. The more she did it without him, however, the quicker she came to the decision that she didn't want to do it if it meant she wouldn't be able to have him in her corner.

Her first show was coming up and she decided if he didn't feel comfortable supporting what she was doing, she would let her first show be her last.

The other woman snatched up the glass pie dish.

"His favorite, cherry." Desi sang hoping to get past the troll tolling the bridge. Desi wouldn't be surprised if his sister was the reason he wasn't returning her calls. It'd been well over a month since he had gotten out of the hospital.

She had been in Houston ironing out some final things with her mother's estate, which was clearing out her mother's home and selling all of her belongings. It was a hard thing to do, but good to do. It was closure for that final page in the chapter that was her mother's living legacy. The memories, however, would last and she was determined to make sure her children knew their grandmother.

The woman grumbled, bringing Desi out of her thoughts.

Wayne ignoring her phone calls, texts, and video chat requests made it clear that he was serious about his silence. She figured coming over unannounced was the best chance she had of actually talking to him face to face.

She didn't, however, account for the woman standing before her. Desi looked the woman over, slim built, but had strong sinewy arms and legs. Either way, she was pretty confident she could take the woman down if she had to.

Wayne's sister glared at Desi. "I see right through you. You ruined him. He might never ride again. You know that's who he is, right? He lives for riding—"

"Joey Lou, get on outta here."

The woman turned on her sibling. "What? I'm wrong? It's her fault your ass is in a sling. If she'd've—"

"Stop." He moved his sister out of the way and stood in the open door. Desi's insides moved at the sight of him, mixed feelings washing over her. "I made a choice and I'd do it again. Now get outta here, please."

His sister let out a breath while boring holes into the side of his head with her glare. She huffed after a while. "Reckon I better go ahead and get dinner started."

"Can you start by cutting me a slice of that pie?"

"Mom would have your head if she knew you were eating dessert before your meal. You want ice cream with it too?"

"Is there any other way to have it?"

The woman smiled begrudgingly, leaving the porch and walking into the house.

They were alone.

187

"It's still warm." Desi struggled to hold back the tears burning behind her eyes. He looked like hell but still held his roguish charm. He had remnants of a black eye and a bruised cheek. His arm was out of sight, only because it was in a blue sling.

"Perfect." They just stared at each other for a long moment, her noticing things about him that she forgot because of the time lapse.

He leaned on the door frame his body holding the thing open.

He exhaled and looked at his feet then back up at her from under his lashes. "You ain't never answer me when I asked back at the hospital what you were doin' in that ring to begin with. 'Specially after you said you were done with it all."

She swallowed knowing this would come up but didn't know it would be so soon. "I-I know I broke the promise I made back in L.A and I'm sorry for that. I had no intentions of going back on my word."

"Hmm," he exhaled. "Well then, why did you?"

"I-I was in the stands like planned eatin' nachos and cheerin' like all the others. Rage came out the holding pen with a vengeance, buckin' and turnin' wild like nothin' we ain't never seen before. You were holdin' on though rolling with him goddamn he couldn't shake you." She smiled recalling how excited she'd been counting down with the rest of the crowd. "Everyone erupted in cheers you beat the time that any Rage rider had ever gotten. The crowd was mad, but I noticed something was off. You were stuck to him tryin' to get loose, but you couldn't. Your arm twisted funny when he finally got you off him made my stomach turn seein' it. On top of that, you caught the top of his head, flew across the arena like a rag doll." She sucked in her breath reliving the terror all over again. She swallowed a thick blockage in her throat. "You were free, but I saw he wasn't done with you." Her attention was focused on the ground as she pulled up the memory like it was second nature to breathing. She'd had her share of nightmares that didn't all turn out the way reality had it. "The other clowns were trying, but nothing was working. You were struggling to stand up, to get out, but you kept fallin' down. I-I just acted. I didn't think—"

"Des—"

"I couldn't just sit back." The same panic she felt sitting in those stands with Wayne struggling to stand, trying to limp out of the ring, filled her up. "I-I couldn't just stand there and watch someone else I loved be taken from me."

She saw the physical impact of her words when they crashed into him. "S-someone you love?" She finally met his eyes filled with deep, swirling emotions: wonder maybe, confusion, uncertainty.

She frowned. "Well, yes. Of course I love you. You're my man."

Her insides lit up when his handsome face pulled into a crooked smirk. "I'm what?" He adjusted his lean on the frame.

She rolled her eyes recognizing the play in his voice. "You're my man."

"Mmm," he grumbled, nodding his head. "Is that right?"

"Mhm." She crossed her hands over her chest wanting to approach him, but uncertain if he was ready for that. She looked up at him from under her lashes still standing at the bottom step. "Surely you have to know that I love you."

He laughed the low reverberations of his amusement seeming to echo inside her mind and send jolts of joy and peace into her soul. "Of course you do. I'm a lovable kind of guy."

She giggled. "Wayne."

"Pretty sure you ain't never said it though." He pushed away from the frame and stepped aside opening up a space that led into the house. "Where are my manners? Come on in."

"I didn't know you even knew the word manners." She walked past him and into the porch.

She yipped when he grabbed her ass. "Didn't say I had many of 'em."

She turned to face him, her smile quickly sobered as she took him in again. "How are you?" She examined him before turning and walking from the porch into the house.

"Just had a broken arm which is quick on the mend. Got the cast off a couple days ago. This sling here is really a part of therapy. Everything else is superficial. I'll be fine. Lived through worse." He smiled up at her and she smiled back.

"Very good, and correct use of the word worse, might I add."

"What can I say, I had a good teacher." He cast his amusement down to look at his boots. "I, uh, I wanted to see you sooner, but with how we left things I've been havin' a hard time figuring stuff out. How're things going with your mom's stuff? Is it all taken care of? I told Kyle if you needed anything--"

She placed her fingers tips over his lips the energy of the simple touch sent shockwaves of heat and electricity through her body. "I know. I got the message. Everything has been taken care of except for the house. Derrick is putting it on the market. I'm more concerned about you."

His eyebrows pulled into a deep frown. "Damn bull's an ornery bastard. Everyone knows that. I just couldn't let this happen to you."

"I appreciate your heroism, but you've seen me in action." She presented a shy smile, going over every bit of the series of events that had led him to the hospital.

"Maybe, but he had that special look in his eyes." Wayne took a deep breath in, his eyes focused on the ground. "Truth is, I'm not sorry." He reached out and cupped her cheek with his good arm. He held her eyes for a long time, an intense look in his. "I ain't never felt fear like that. Seeing him close in on you. I don't think I've ever cared about anyone like I care about you."

Her chest pressed on itself. "I'm sorry you went through that, the pain, the possibility of ending your career." She walked a few paces away, wondering how to say what she was thinking. She wasn't sure how he would take it with everything that had gone down.

"What? What is it?"

She released the breath she didn't realize she was holding. "I can't regret the time I spent in that pen. It's the rush, the... the art of it all. There's no way to overpower the creature. All I can hope to do is outsmart him. I have to use what I thought I lost—" She looked at Wayne with tears threatening to fall from her eyes. "I thought I lost it. That it was all a waste."

"What?"

"My tumbling skills, my gymnastics stuff. Another thing I'd lost when I lost my dad." She turned away from him as memories of her father helping her with flips, floated through her mind. "I don't want to waste those skills, but I also don't want you worrying about me like you did.

He exhaled stuffing his hands in his pockets. "The Matador thing at the Stadium in a couple days?"

She nodded hope floating in her chest. She checked it recalling the deal she made with herself. "I think it'll be a good way for me to still be in the pen, having fun with my stunting, and do it all without the danger of the bulls." She glanced up at him from under her lashes, trying to gauge his reaction, but there wasn't one.

The air was thick.

Had she made him angry even bringing it up, even considering it? Was this all a mistake? "If you don't think it's—"

"You need this, don't you?" He looked down at his feet then back up at her.

She swallowed and gnawed on her lower lip as she nodded her head.

His eyes fell to her mouth and lingered there. "Will it satisfy you?" he wanted to know, taking a couple steps toward her.

She nodded. "I-I think so?"

He took a deep breath and let it go, coming to stand a foot away. "Will it satiate your desire for the thrilling excitement of the pen?" He grabbed the nape of her neck with his good arm, pulling her closer to him. Jittering heat snaked around her body at the pent up energy she had for him. He pressed her lips to his and held her there until she slanted toward his face, wanting more, a deeper connection.

Both their attention was suddenly drawn to his sister standing in the archway holding the cherry pie.

*

"Looks like you don't need the pie after all."

Wayne grumbled at the interruption. Always with the worst timing that sister of his. "Leave, Joey Lou."

She rolled her eyes and turned.

"No, hand over the pie and go, and not to the kitchen. Leave the house." His mouth was watering maybe for the pie maybe for the woman who brought it. He wasn't sure which it was and he could care less about the details.

"Ew," the woman whispered and walked out the front door. She held up a middle finger. "I'm taking the damn pie." She put a spoonful in her mouth and grumbled something under her breath before taking another bite.

After his sister was out of sight he turned his attention back to Desi. Damn she was beautiful. HIs body, for the first time in a month

191

and half felt energized, ready to take on anything. "Joey Lou was pushin' me to go to your show this friday, but I can't."

She frowned with a nod. He tipped her face up to meet his gaze. "Ain't cause I wouldn't. I've got some meetin' up in Dallas. Damn city rats trynna have me dancin' around like a pansy on some talk shows or somethin' like that. Could you imagine it?"

She nodded. "I understand."

He laughed when she whispered his name, probably because his hands were wanderin' and had formed over the curve of her ass. His more manly anatomy had not trouble responding to the sensual sound. With all that had gone down all he wanted was to have his woman in his arms for the next twenty-four hours.

Desi leaned into him then gasped when he pulled up the hem of her dress, moved her panties aside and stroked her. "Enough about all that for now. All I really want is to be with my girl." He took her lips as if he'd never get to kiss the woman again. Her lips were so soft just like everything else about her sweet body. Soft yet firm. He didn't have a clue how she did it but he was grateful for it.

He pulled away.

"What?" Her brows were furrowed, and concern distorted her symmetrical features. He straightened to a full stand and unbuckled his jeans then pushed them and his boxers over his hips, pulling the shirt over his head. There was no sense in playing around. He retrieved a condom from his back pocket, ripped it open and rolled it over his cock.

She was watching him, seeming to be in disbelief. She would believe in a moment. He kissed her and laid her on the couch so he could settle between her legs.

"Wayne," she whined.

He kissed her mouth, jaw, nibbled her ear. He heard her breath catch when he slid more of his cock between her dripping wet lower lips. "You know what," he whispered in her ear.

She wrapped her leg over his hips, taking him all the way to the hilt. He bit his tongue to stop himself from calling out to the baby Jesus and getting a one-way ticket to hell. He moved his hips in and out of her slick opening. "Fucking God!" he moaned. Hell, he was probably already going to hell anyway with the lifestyle he lived before his Desi came along.

192

He pulled away a little, still moving his hips at a steady pace, to see her beautiful face poised in a look of pleasure. Her eyes were closed, her inky lashes resting on her cheeks. He picked up the pace and watched her face contort, her eyebrows furrow, her full lips part. He grabbed her breast and pinched the nipple.

He slowed the pace, examining his handiwork. He pretty pink dress was pulled up to her waist, the neckline stretched down under her supple breasts, which were exposed because the bra was unclasped and hanging useless to the sides. Strands of her dense hair had escaped the updo. He reached out and wrapped his finger around one of her tiny twisted strands.

She grabbed his hand and pressed a kiss to the palm before she met his eyes with a devious expression. She formed his hand over her breast and bit her lower lip.

Fuck!

He framed her face between his arms and drove into her with one sure purpose. Her thighs tightened around his hips. He held her ass at just the right— yep right there. "Oh shit. Shit, shit fuck," he ground out between clenched teeth.

A familiar overwhelming feeling started building inside him, making him feel out of control. There was no where for him to go, nothing for him to do besides let go of all that had happened.

His smooth thrusts turned staggered and jerky before he was consumed by sensation, much like the woman below him.

He wanted her.

He wanted her to display his photo on her mantel, to smile with her heart when she gazed up at him. She had him, whether she wanted him or not. All of him too. The fiendish miscreant that he was and whatever else they'd shape him into.

| 40 | The Mad Matador |

Desi took a deep breath with her arms spread wide as the audience cheered after her first performance as the Mad Matador. She was nervous like all hell, but excitement streaked through her body, filling her with energy she'd never felt the likes of before.

She was ready, and the show went off without a hitch.

Her thoughts drifted to Wayne. She wished he was there but he was off in Dallas being a celebrity despite his chagrin. She giggled imagining him in an interview completely annoyed, completely uninterested with one word responses.

The past couple days she was leaning hard into the show. Because of that, she hadn't been able to see him since she had dropped the cherry pie off a couple of days before. She missed him and wished he was there to see all that she'd been working towards.

She and her crew jogged out of the pen, the others talking excitedly. She half-heartedly celebrated with them, but instead of going to their tent, she went to Wayne's barn. Ever since he was injured the barn had been empty save for the hay and other assortment of gear. No one used it though. It was as if they were savin' it for him or somethin'.

She chucked the gloves on the ground and flopped down on a bale of hale. She exhaled feeling the exhaustion settle in her body. She wasn't sure her mother found place in her mind, but the woman did. She let her face fall in her palms and tears rushed over her. "I miss you mama." Felt good to release, but the sorrow was unexpected and overwhelming.

194

The days were longer now that summer was upon them and the sun was starting to fall out of the sky.

"My sexy little Mad Matador."

Desi started, standing immediately to her feet. "W-Wayne?" Her insides flipped about itself. "W-what are you doin' here?" She started wiping her eyes profusely.

"My lady had a rodeo I needed to attend. If I can't ride, might as well watch you do some crazy stunts." He pushed off the barn door frame and took a few steps towards her. She looked him up and down and bit her lower lip. He was a sight with his hat covering his dirty blonde hair, clean jeans and plaid shirt. Even the faded bruises on his face couldn't detour from his roguish good looks.

"Not sure how you did Dallas and got to see my show but I'm grateful—" She gasped when he pulled her to him with his newly healed arm.

"Anything for my lady?"

"The corner of her mouth lifted. Anything for your lady, huh?"

He raised an eyebrow as mischief danced in his eyes. "Ifin' you had any questions after you dropped off that pie, then I ain't do my job right."

She laughed looking down at her dirty cowboy boots. Oh no, she had no questions. He grabbed her chin and lifted her eyes to meet his again. She frowned and cocked her head to the side at his somber look.

"You don't know this, but your mama grilled me into the ground."

She frowned. "What?" It didn't sting as much now, hearing her mother mentioned.

"Asked me how many other girls I was fuckin' and why I picked you."

Desi gasped. "What!" She looked mortified.

"Okay, she didn't say fuckin', but same difference. Thing I'm gettin' at is, I told her I chose you because you were the one I wanted. That ain't never gonna change, here that?"

She swallowed with a nod. The mention of her mother still made her waiver a bit. "I miss momma." She didn't try to stop the tears that spilled over the edge of her lips and down her cheeks. She leaned into him and inhaled his scent, which usually had a hay undertone, but all she could smell was his soap. He linked his arms to keep her close. She couldn't make out the soothing words he was saying while he kissed the top of her head, but she liked it. It felt good.

She pulled away a minute to look into his cool grey eyes.

"W-Wayne I—" She sniffled before her head fell. "I missed you these past several weeks. They were really tough with everything going on. It was—" She took in a short breath as if there was a shortage of air. "It was hard p-packin' up Mama's house."

"I know, baby. I'm sorry I wasn't there. Things shouldn't have gone the way they did. I should have been there for you. I'm so sorry." He rested his head on top of her head and rocked her slightly. The motion was soothing.

She pulled away reluctantly needing to look into his eyes. "It's not entirely your fault." She looked down at the dirt floor. "I-I wasn't being fair to you. About the clowning thing that is. If you really don't want me to do it, I won't."

He made her look at him again with a pointer under her chin. "Don't be silly. I loved watchin' you out there. You came alive, pretty Miss Limb."

She looked down and giggled at the name that was kind of a pet name for her now. Strange how things started and where they'd ended up. If not for his relentless pursuit, she'd have missed out on so many truly beautiful moments.

"I missed you more than I care to admit outloud." He tipped her chin up to look at him again. "I've been drivin' Joey Lou right up the wall with all my mopin', as she calls it. Oh, and she damn near ate that entire pie, by the way—"

"Wayne? Wayne Dunbar?!" Their laughter fell off abruptly as both of their attention was brought to the open barn door. "It's him! It's Wayne! Hey Wayne, I have a few questions..."

In rushed a reporter and cameraman followed by a flood of others taking pictures and crowding around everyone talking at once. She couldn't make out any one thing they were saying.

"I'mma kill Liz. Come on!" He grabbed her hand and pulled her out of the barn before they could get too close. He tossed a heavy drum in front of the back door with her help after they struggled to get it closed.

"Did we lose 'em?"

"Prolly not for long." A loud banging on the door sent them running hand in hand. For some odd reason they were laughing like adolescents running for police.

They stopped somewhere between two barns to catch their breath.

"I'm real happy you showed up. It means a lot to me," she told him.

The corner of his mouth lifted. "You mean a lot to me, pretty Miss Limb, and nothing is going to change that."

"LOOK! THERE HE IS!"

"Goddamn it! Been dodgin' these bastards for the past month and a half. Liz sent them here. I know she did, damn ball buster." They took off running again, dodging in and out of barns, granaries and training pens.

They paused between several buildings. "I've got to get my stamina back up," he said, panting.

She looked at him over her shoulder and smirked. "Think you got in a good start the other day."

The corner of his mouth lifted making his moondust eyes sparkle. "Don't start something now."

"Why not?" She approached him with a sultry saunter. "After, we find a place a bit more private, I plan on starting lots of things."

His laughter made her smile. She frowned and started looking around. The corner of her mouth lifted as the perfect plan started to unfold.

"What you thinkin?"

"Do you think you can keep up?" she asked, crossing her arms with a smirk. He pulled away slightly, the corner of his mouth lifted.

"Well, my pretty little matador, that almost sounds like a challenge." He pulled her close and set a simple kiss on her lips.

She laughed, slipping out of his arms then hopped up onto an old oil canister. "Well, are you up for the challenge? Not sure if you can pull it off with a busted up arm."

"HERE! HE'S OVER HERE!"

She didn't wait for him to respond, only hopped up on to the barn's roof, and he followed.

They ran over rooftops, jumping over haylofts, between training pens and holding barns. Eventually, they found themselves on a tin roof under a clear night sky.

They set down carefully the rodeo and all that came with it, including the annoying reporters, were off in the distance, white noise in their solace.

It felt like something out of her chapter as a teen. Lying on the roof with a boy under the stars, 'cept he wasn't a boy. She glanced over at Wayne who was looking up at the sky for a moment before he turned his head to the side to gaze at her.

He offered his hand, palm up, and without thinking she slid her hand in his. He smiled over at her before he lifted her hand to his mouth and kissed it. She enjoyed his fingers tangling with hers in a gentle mindless way.

She brought her attention back up to the sky. "You think my mom's seeing the same night sky?"

He exhaled and glanced over at her. "Actually, I think she is a star."

"Yeah." She smiled and let a warm contemplative silence settle between them.

"She really liked looking out at the night sky," Desi said smiling, recalling a memory. "Said she felt closer to God because she knew how small she was. Small and infinitely significant."

"Mmm," he said thoughtfully. "Did she have a favorite constellation?"

"Of course. Hers was Orion. I think it's because he's pretty easy to find." She giggled searching the sky for her quiry. "Look, there he is." She pointed her left hand at the sky, tracing the bright dots, and was distracted by a bright gleam that wasn't a star. She frowned, sitting up and examining her hand.

Wayne set up beside her, but her gaze was locked on the large diamond that he had, somewhere in all of this, slipped onto her ring finger. After she sat there staring at it for a long period of time, he cleared his throat.

"Suppose I should have asked you first before putting it on your finger. I-I can't never manage to do things in the right order. Pretty Miss Desiree Limb, will you—"

His words got caught in his throat when she dove on him, smashing their mouths together. His face was in her palms and his arm found her slender waist with ease. She pulled away, his eyes catching all the lights making them look like the night sky with the stars dancing there in them. "Would I be correct in assuming that means you accept?" he asked, with a faint smile on his face before he stroked her cheek.

She brushed her fingers along his jaw with her left hand and paused a moment to look at the ring before the corner of her mouth pulled up and she gazed down at him again this time with a frown. "It does seem to pose a problem."

The corner of his mouth lifted as he reached up and cupped her cheek. "Yeah? What's that?"

"Suppose you'll have to figure out something else to call me besides Pretty Miss Limb," she said softly melting at the adoration and love she saw swimming in his heavy lidded eyes.

His laughter started deep in his chest and filled her ears with his amusement. "I reckon, Sexy Mrs. Dunbar has a nice ring to it too."

The End

If you liked *Impossible Rogue*, please provide a review via email, amazon or any other distribution outlet that you purchased you copy:

alex@alexandriaashcroft.com

http://www.alexandriaashcroft.com

You have no idea how much I appreciate you taking the time to write a review. It really helps other readers find my work!

I LISTEN TO MY READERS AND VALUE YOUR OPINION, SO TELL ME WHAT YOU WANT TO READ NEXT!.

STORY QUESTIONS:

Who was your favorite character?

Have you or would you ever attend a rodeo?

Do you think Wayne & Desi make a good match?

Do you think the story had a satisfactory ending?

Email me your answers at alex@alexandriaashcroft.com

The most creative/interesting answers get a prize!!

Alexandria Ashcroft is a Romance and Erotic Romance author. Her stories, under this pen name, focus on deep character development that highlight emotionally rich personas in vibrant settings. In addition to writing, she is a mother of one robust and opinionated toddler, is a designer in the building construction industry, and is also an avid traveler. She currently resides in the midwest United States; however, with all her heart and mind, is planning her next destination for travel and adventure. "I've so many places to go, to see," she says. "And each place imprints a unique brand on me as an individual and on my writing. There are so many stories to tell. The only limitation is time. Where do you want to travel next?"

Teasing the Palate (Book 1: Dirty Wine Series)

A woman stops at a winery on her way to share a weekend with her girl friends. Intrigued by the winery owner's handsome face and sturdy build, she decides to sample more than just the fermented grapes.

Sinnful (Book 1: Devil Sinn M.C. Series)

After losing her white knight and the idealistic life she thought she wanted, Lacey reunites with the man whose very breath steals her own. His father's death puts him in a reluctant position of power and past transgressions place him and his brethren on the peak of war.

Dream Catcher (Book 1: Darkest Hour Collection)

An ancient creature said to have the power to rouse those stuck in the dream plane is coaxed out of isolation by a young woman trying to save her sister who is stuck in a nightmare, an endless void searching for answers. From the shadows of her unconscious mind he lurks, but he's not the only one she feels on the fringes of her mind, quiet, terrifying and disturbingly close.

LET'S CONNECT!

I honestly enjoy hearing from you!

Join my Little Black Dress subscription service. It's free and you get access to FREE stories, entered into giveaways, and more. HOLD the spamming emails. I don't like those either.

Shoot me an email:

alex@alexandriaashcroft.com

Check out my website:

www.alexandriaashcroft.com

Keep up with what I'm doing! Win free merch & Books by following me on:

#1 Instagram AlexandriaAshcroft

#2 Youtube AlexandriaAshcroft

#3 Twitter @AlexandriaAshe

| Facebook | | Wattpad |

"If they want you, they will consistently show you how precious your heart is to them."

- Alex

www.ingramcontent.com/pod-product-compliance
Lightning Source LLC
Chambersburg PA
CBHW032126170626
46808CB00006B/2119